In *Confessions to a Stranger*, Danielle Grandinetti weaves a tale that is at once mysterious, suspenseful, romantic, and inspiring ... Filled with truths that made me ponder my own life, this novel is a lovely start to what is sure to be a wonderful series!

—Heidi Chiavaroli,
Carol Award-Winning Author of *The Orchard House*

Danielle Grandinetti has crafted a wonderful tale of suspense and romance that will keep you on the edge of your seat. With well-drawn characters authentic to the era, a gripping plot, and a strong message of hope, *Confessions to a Stranger* is a read I recommend!

—Misty M. Beller,
USA Today bestselling author of the Sisters of the Rockies

A Strike to the Heart is a compelling story. From the very first page, I was immersed into the thrilling action and remained gripped with intrigue until the satisfying ending. The romance escalated right along with the winding plot, creating a layered mystery that is sure to delight readers.

—Rachel Scott McDaniel,
Award-winning author of *The Mobster's Daughter*

Riveting from the first scene, *As Silent as the Night* offers a unique, edge-of-your-seat Christmas read ... A beautiful, gripping, and romantically suspenseful Christmas story you wouldn't be able to put down if you tried.

—Chautona Havig,
Author of *The Stars of New Cheltenham*

The Neighbor and the Gifts is a poignant tale that transforms a familiar carol into a stirring journey of faith, love, and danger ... For readers who love historical romance, mystery, and want a deeper meaning in their holiday stories—this one's for you.

—Natalie Walters,
bestselling and award-winning author of *Living Lies* and the *SNAP Agency* series

Escape with the Prodigal

**Discover the Foundation
of Danielle's Bookish World**

Harbored in Crow's Nest
Confessions to a Stranger
Refuge for the Archaeologist
Escape with the Prodigal
Relying on the Enemy
Sheltered by the Doctor
Investigation of a Journalist

Bridge: His Boss's Little Sister

Unexpected Protectors
To Stand in the Breach
A Strike to the Heart
As Silent as the Night

For a complete list, visit
daniellegrandinetti.com/books

Escape with the Prodigal

Danielle Grandinetti

Hearth Spot Press

In memory of my late
grandfather,
Carl Reinhold

a Wisconsin dairy farmer
who worked for a lumber
company during several
winters

It was meet that we should make merry, and be glad:

for this thy brother was dead, and is alive again; and

was lost, and is found.

Luke 15:32, KJV

CHAPTER ONE

Northern Wisconsin
Thursday, December 18, 1930

Still a week until Christmas and Patrick Martins's gloved fingers were nearly frozen. He flexed them on the handle of the crosscut saw he shared with his sister's friend, Kyle Docherty. Kyle's stocking cap hid his shaggy strawberry-blond hair but not his wind-burned ears.

They'd already notched one side of the hardwood tree to control the direction of its descent. Now they bit the teeth of the saw into the tree's opposite side. Back and forth they drew the saw. Sweat gathered on Patrick's back. His arm muscles burned, the pain the only feeling that reminded him he was alive.

"Timber!" The voice of his brother, David, had Patrick and Kyle pausing their work.

The tall tree Patrick's brother had cut with his lumber partner teetered before cleanly crashing to the ground. Kyle tugged their saw to get it moving again, but while they worked, Patrick watched as a handful of men attacked the felled tree. They would trim the branches until only the trunk was left. Then they'd drag it over to the sled wagon where a pulley system lifted the log to the top of the horse-drawn sleigh that would take the towering load down the icy road to the rail line.

Their foreman, Emyr Hughes, directed the loading. He owned the team of four draft horses that pulled the sleigh. Stories told how he and the owner of the Alaric Lumber Company, Arthur Alaric, grew up together. While Alaric founded the lumber company, Hughes kept it running. He swore like a taskmaster, drank like Patrick's father, and had a beautiful daughter Patrick—and every other lumberman, except saintly David—had a difficult time keeping his eyes off of.

"Put yer mind back on the tree, Martins," Kyle grouched, his Scottish brogue accentuated by his grumpiness. "You're going to get us killed."

Patrick rolled his eyes. Yes, lumbering was dangerous. Yes, a lumberman needed to keep focused so he didn't get hurt. But, frankly, Patrick liked the danger, the thrill. It reached past the numbness that had calloused his heart since his mother died when he was a kid.

"I aim to get home to Sam," Kyle muttered. Usually, he had an easy smile on that freckled face of his, but not today.

"What was that?" Patrick shoved the saw back at Kyle, causing him to *oomph*.

Kyle sent the saw back just as hard. "You know how I feel about her."

Just now, Patrick didn't care. He wasn't about to let another man destroy his sister's life, as their father continued to do. "You stay away from her, you understand? Samantha deserves better than you."

The man was a fisherman, working in the lumber camps to earn a living during the offseason. Like David. But Patrick didn't need the money, not really. He had no needs. Only a quest to stay occupied. However, Kyle and David, risking life and limb out here, showed how a girl could turn a man's head.

Women made a man do things he regretted. Not to mention the responsibility they required. Patrick shivered. Never would he tie himself to someone who needed that of him. No duty meant no reason to fail. As his father did. Because he would never be like his father.

"Martins!"

A crack brought Patrick's head around faster than Kyle's shout. When had they cut through the trunk?

"Timber!" Kyle yanked the saw from Patrick's hands and they dodged the falling tree.

The tall giant of the forest tipped, tipped, caught. Its wide-reaching branches tangled with those around it. Then it snapped, dropping the trunk to the ground and leaving the large crown caught in the treetops. A widowmaker.

The cold from Patrick's fingers shot through his body. Had his inattention done this?

"What in blazes is going on here?" Hughes stomped over. The man was as thick as he was tall, with a graying blond beard that covered his chest and a knit hat that smashed down a wavy mane.

The skin around his eyes looked like wrinkled leather, but his eyes themselves were as dark as coal. Patrick involuntarily took a step back.

Kyle stepped forward. "Sir, it's my—"

"Accidents happen." Patrick cut him off. He might not approve of Kyle calling on his little sister, but he wouldn't let him take the blame for something that wasn't his fault.

"Accidents will get you killed, Martins." Hughes seemed to grow.

Patrick squared his shoulders and refused to show the unease that threatened to choke him.

"Instead of casting blame, let's get that tree down." David. Always the big brother coming to his rescue.

Hughes didn't blink. "Fine. Get it down. This young pup is on mess clean-up tonight."

Patrick clenched his teeth. He wouldn't let the big man get a visible reaction out of him.

"Come on." David pulled Patrick's shoulder. "Let's get to work."

Hughes would make Patrick move first, so he had no choice but to let David lead him to the ropes they had ready for just such an occasion. He hated the powerless feeling that rolled through him. It reminded him too much of when his mother died and his father resigned from being a dad. There had been nothing he could do to stop his mother's death or his father's leaving, and there was nothing he could do to stop Hughes from shoving his superiority around.

He slammed his palm into a tree. A worthless action that only caused his hand to ache.

"Hey." David grabbed his arm. "Get a hold on yourself, Patrick, or you'll get tossed out. Maybe get the rest of us in trouble too. Or worse. These things aren't called a widowmaker because it's a cute name. That branch could get loose and kill someone. Understand?"

"Yes, Dad." Patrick glared at his older brother. The old resentment that David'd had to take over a parental role rose up strong.

David closed his eyes on a sigh. "I'm not arguing with you. Do your job."

"Fine. Send me up." A widowmaker didn't scare him because he had no one depending on him. If he was hurt, if he died, he left behind no one who needed him.

Meredith Hughes pressed her fists into her aching back before bending over to pull yet another tray of biscuits out of the oven. "That's the last of them, Mrs. Nelson."

"Wonderful." The thin, older lady held out a wooden spoon. "Come taste this. I fear it's more watery than I hoped. Not even Christmas and I'm already running low on herbs. It's going to be a long winter at this rate."

Meri dumped the biscuits into a basket, covered them with a cloth, then took the spoon from the cook. "You know how to make the simplest meal taste like home. I'm sure it's wonderful."

"Pish-posh. You can flatter a fly." But Mrs. Nelson watched closely as Meri sipped a sample of the bubbling stew.

"Delicious." And Meri was telling the truth. Or maybe she was just hungry. She was always hungry these days. "Are the herbs truly running low already?"

"Yes, dear. Everything we have left is what I managed to grow over the summer, and it wasn't much."

Meri tried to push away the fear that hovered close to the surface. "I overheard Father saying the company might be near bankruptcy because of the crash."

"I have heard the same. Holt Lumber closed their camp last year. I don't see how Alaric will survive if the larger companies have all died out or moved west."

"Where will you go if you don't work here?" Meri busied herself with setting the coffee on the stove despite her shaky fingers. The men would be coming to mess cold and hungry from a day in the forest, or what was left of it. There were so few pockets of trees left in Wisconsin, the lumber companies had been selling off their cut-over land.

Mrs. Nelson rested her hands on her narrow hips, surveying her domain. "Mr. Nelson and I aren't getting any younger, and we don't see much of our grandchildren. With her husband gone, perhaps we'll move to Crow's Nest to be closer to our daughter."

"Crow's Nest?"

"It's a small fishing town on Lake Michigan." She waved a hand toward the forest. "You know those lumberjacks, David Martins, his brother Patrick, and their friend Kyle? They're from Crow's Nest. Mr. Nelson got them jobs up here for the season."

She knew the faces that went to those names. The clean-shaven David who moved with such ease. Kyle, who dominated the vocals during the Saturday night singalongs. And Patrick. So handsome with that blond scruff he called a beard.

An uncomfortable feeling of jealousy spurted through her. What would it be like to have family or friends go out of their way to help? She'd give her last penny to have someone champion her, especially after Leo died so unexpectedly this summer, leaving her in such a precarious state.

"It's normal to get more emotional, you know." Mrs. Nelson gave her an understanding smile. "Are you sure you have nowhere else to stay for the winter?"

Tears pressed her eyes, and she kept her head ducked while she arranged the food line. "Nowhere, even if Father let me leave." And when he found out her mistake? She'd be at the mercy of his storied temper once again.

Cold air swept through the mess hall as the first wave of lumberjacks effectively ended their conversation and banished her emotion. Mrs. Nelson filled bowls with stew, and Meri added a biscuit and mug of coffee before handing a meal to each man as they filed past. Meri found herself paying closer attention to David Martins and his friend Kyle as they took their trays from her, and noting that David's brother Patrick was not with them. Patrick was definitely the most handsome of the trio—not that she cared.

In past years, she would occasionally flirt with the lumberjacks, even if her father put the fear of him into the men if they should so much as smile at her. Leo had disregarded Father's warning, and look where that got them. Now she still smiled at the jacks, but it was a mask to hide behind.

She forced a brighter smile for her father as he went through the line, but he ignored her. Ever since Mama died when she was little, he'd ignored her, unless she was a target of his temper. Why couldn't she escape somewhere? Maybe Mrs. Nelson would let her go with her and Mr. Nelson to this Crow's Nest place. Except, by then, when the spring thaw had melted the ice and the logging season ended, it would be too late.

"Can I get a cup?"

Meri jerked her head up to find Patrick across from her, his eyes twinkling. "Of course." She poured coffee into a mug. Why did the man have to be more handsome than the other jacks? Why was she even thinking that way? Coffee splashed on her skin. *Ow!*

The slightest frown showed he'd seen her discomfort despite her attempt to surreptitiously wipe her hand on her apron. But he only nodded and went to join the other men.

"That's the last of them." Mrs. Nelson handed her a damp cloth. "Go wipe down the tables as the men leave, and let them know we have a small portion left for seconds."

"Yes, ma'am." Meri scurried into the large mess hall. Two long tables, with benches on either side stretched the length of the room. She stayed on the periphery, careful to keep her distance from the men. A touch from one always sent her father into a rage, if he saw it.

A few jacks went back to the kitchen for seconds, but most moseyed out into the darkness. She stacked the empty bowls and turned back to the kitchen only to catch her toe on the end of the bench. She stumbled, but two muscular arms caught her before she fell.

"Easy there." Patrick.

Her cheeks flamed hot.

He set up her upright, his hand skimming her waist in a protective way. Questions popped into his eyes, transforming to concern, as he glanced at her belly. Her heartbeat jumped to triple time. He'd figured out her secret.

CHAPTER TWO

Patrick snatched his hands away from Meredith Hughes. The red of her cheeks, the way she avoided his gaze, told him he guessed right. His boss's daughter was expecting a child.

And, as far as he knew, she wasn't married. He glanced at her left hand, and she shifted the other to cover it while still holding the stack of bowls. Nope. Not married.

What did he do now? He'd only meant to steady her, not reveal her secret. Not that she'd be able to hide it for long, considering he, a confirmed bachelor, had noticed. Of course, he wasn't oblivious to such issues since his grandmother had taken in enough needy people over the years, including a couple of unwed mothers.

"Please don't say anything." Her green eyes shimmered. "Don't tell my father."

He swallowed an unsavory phrase he'd learned from working among the fishermen back home. "Does anyone else know?"

"Mrs. Nelson."

His shoulders relaxed. The Nelsons got him this job, thanks to David's connection with their daughter, Marian, or rather, Marian's brother-in-law. "They're good people. She'll watch out for you."

Yet her chin trembled.

He should put distance between them before the straggling lumberjacks got too curious. The last thing he needed was Emyr Hughes on his case. The man was already mad at him for the widowmaker this afternoon. Even if Patrick had safely cut the thing out of the branches that had caught it.

"Your dad ordered me to help with mess clean-up tonight. I'll deliver these to Mrs. Nelson." He forced a smile and took the bowls from her, making quick strides into the kitchen.

"What are you doing here, Patrick?" Mrs. Nelson spared him a smile while elbow deep in a washbasin.

"Ordered to help, ma'am." He glanced back to see if Meredith had followed. She hadn't. Patrick dunked the stack of bowls, using the excuse to lean close to Mrs. Nelson's ear. "Miss Hughes told me that you know. She can't hide for long. Isn't there some place she can go?"

Mrs. Nelson crossed her arms, wet hands and all. "Where, pray tell, do you think she can go when in the middle of winter? This situation has swallowed the poor girl whole. And don't you dare think of making it worse."

He didn't have an answer, however as soon as the jacks found out, her reputation would be ruined. And when her father learned of it? "We need to get her out of here." Urgency spat the words from his mouth.

"We?" Mrs. Nelson studied him for a long moment, as if measuring his soul. He had no doubt she'd find him wanting. Everyone else did.

"I know fathers." He sure had a rotten one. Patrick blew out a breath. If only he didn't know with such certainty how Meredith's father would react when he found out. And unless they—not *they*, *he* wasn't getting involved—unless Meredith got out of the lumber camp as soon as possible, it was a matter of *when*, not *if*, Hughes discovered the truth. Patrick rubbed his chest, hating the emotion clanging against the bars around his heart.

"You're right about her father, but this is Meri's decision." Mrs. Nelson waved him away. "Best keep this to yourself and forget you know about it."

"My grandmother has taken in women plenty of times." Why wasn't he taking the life preserver Mrs. Nelson threw him? The ability to walk away from responsibility with a clear conscience? "Grandma won't blink at Miss Hughes' ... condition."

"I'll consider mentioning it." Mrs. Nelson dunked her hands into the washbasin. "Now get back to work."

Patrick reentered the mess hall, his gaze immediately going to where Meredith gathered bowls on the opposite side. The large room was empty now. He studied her more closely. She grimaced as she stretched her back. A twist revealed the slight bump beneath her apron. He knew to look for these things now, but soon other men would notice them too. Men who had wives back home, wives who had children.

And what of her child's father?

He stacked bowls on the nearest table more roughly than necessary. Why did the situation make him angry? It was none of his business, and Mrs. Nelson wanted him to butt out. Besides, simply knowing about Meredith's condition added an unnecessary weight to his shoulders.

"Mr. Martins? Patrick?" Meredith appeared beside him. How had he stacked bowls from half the table already? "You're angry." *At me?* He heard her unspoken question, and he winced. He'd never show anger toward a vulnerable woman.

"No. Not at you."

She looked so small and scared that it took him back to those days after his mom died and his father left. His sister had worn the same expression. But Patrick didn't see Meredith as a little sister and attraction had him wanting to comfort her. Maybe … hug her?

What was with him! And how unwelcome such an action would be to her. He didn't want her to think he considered her a wanton woman. "What of the child's father?" The question leapt out.

Resignation dropped her shoulders. "Alaric keeps a small crew on over the summer, including the Nelsons and my dad. That's how I met Leo."

Leo? None of the other lumberjacks were named Leo.

"We dated secretly because, well, you know my father. Finally, Leo got up the nerve to ask permission to marry me. Father was relieved, happy to pawn me off onto someone else."

"Surely not." Yet even as he said the words, he knew it was true. Men like Emyr Hughes saw a woman—a daughter—as a burden. Shame washed over him. Was he any different from Hughes if he considered women were a responsibility he didn't want?

"He said it to my face, and I was so distraught … well, I let Leo … and then he died in a logging accident." She hugged the bowls to herself. "I learned a couple weeks later, thanks to Mrs. Nelson, that I did not have a stomach bug. I hoped Father would let me skip this winter's camp, but after Leo's death, he refused to let me out of his sight. One minute I'm a burden, the next he won't be rid of me, and exactly when I want to hide."

Patrick worked his jaw. He knew about hiding. It was all he'd done as a kid when his father was in one of his drunken states. Besides, being a middle child had allowed him to hide even better. David had taken the brunt. Maybe he was too hard on his older brother.

"I'm afraid, Patrick, and I don't know why I'm telling you this except that I've been holding the story to myself these past five months, and—"

"I'm glad you told me." Not that he knew what to do with this information. And if Hughes caught him talking to Meredith, he'd be skinned alive.

"Thank you, Patrick Martins." Again her eyes shimmered. "Thank you for not casting judgment."

He took a step back. "Why on earth would I do that?"

"Isn't that what we expect everyone else will do to me?"

She was right. And there wasn't a thing either of them could do about it.

That night, with her father passed out and snoring loudly behind his partition, Meri lit a candle nub and held it over her Bible. Ever since she learned she'd be a mother, she'd been drawn back to this book. Her father hated it, but she remembered her mother reading from it and drew comfort from the memory. And the words. Despite the situation she found herself in, she felt God's care over her. His forgiveness, if not His understanding. At least in these quiet moments, she did.

She tugged her blanket around her shoulders. With only a week until Christmas, and being in her current condition, she felt close to the story of Mary and had read it every night this month. Again, she turned to the first chapter of Luke. *And Mary said, My soul doth magnify the Lord, And my spirit hath rejoiced in God my Saviour. For he hath regarded the low—*

"What are you doing?" Father slapped aside the partition that hid her bed from the rest of the cabin.

She snapped her Bible closed and used it as a shield over her belly.

"I told you I don't want to see that book in my house." He yanked the Bible away, and in her effort not to light her bed on fire with the candle, she failed to cover her middle. Her father stared at her, his face turning purple in the light.

Emotion clogged her throat. "Father, please."

"Who did this to you?" he roared. The stale alcohol on his breath churned her nausea. "I saw you talking with that Martins boy today. It was him, wasn't it?"

"Patrick? No!"

"Patrick, is it?" he shouted at her. "We'll see about that."

He stormed through the cabin, and Meredith leapt after him. "Father, if you would listen—" His backhand silenced her as it sent her flying toward the woodstove that warmed the small place.

"Patrick Martins is an insolent pup, and he's going to pay for what he did to you."

Meri pressed a shaking hand to her raw cheek. She couldn't let Patrick reap consequences for something that wasn't his fault. His only crime was his kindness toward her.

By the time she got to her feet and shoved her arms through her coat to cover her nightgown, her father's bellow reached her ears from across the camp. "Martins! Get out here. Face me like a man."

The Nelsons and Father had individual cabins at the top of the semicircle, the lumberjacks in the long, low building on the west, the mess hall and stables on the east. The clearing in the center was a stomped-down area covered in frozen divots and ice. She plunged across, her feet skidding beneath her. Her hair tossed in her face by the wind.

Meri lost her balance, and her feet slipped from beneath her. She landed hard on her hip, but pushed to her feet. Someone called her name from behind, likely Mrs. Nelson. Still, she pressed on, following her father through the open door of the bunkhouse.

"Martins, you're going to answer for what you did to my daughter." Her father's slurred growl echoed in the low-ceilinged room.

"What are you accusing my brother of?" Patrick's brother, David, faced her father. "You're drunk, Mr. Hughes. Let me—"

No, no, she couldn't let even more people suffer for her mistakes. "Father." A host of eyes turned toward her, and she froze. What had she thought to prove, coming to the men's bunkhouse dressed only in her coat and nightgown?

"What are you doing here?" Her father spun on her, thunder in his voice and rage in his eyes.

All her bluster, her ready defense of Patrick, tangled in her throat.

Father advanced, his breath stale as it blew across her face. "Do you make a habit of coming into my men's sleeping quarters? Why am I here to defend you? You deserve what happened to you. You—" He raised his hand to strike her, but the blow never landed. At least on her.

Patrick blocked her father. "Any man who dares hit a woman doesn't deserve—"

The strike landed this time, not a slap, but a fist to Patrick's jaw. He stumbled and Meredith caught him. And then he was shoving her away. Toward the door. Cold air strangled her. Her boot caught an ice chunk. A strong arm caught her before her knees hit the ground.

"Meredith, we need to move." Patrick set her on her feet and pushed her into a run along the side of the bunkhouse.

The hammer click of a gun told her why.

"You better run!" Her father's voice chased them. "You're no longer my daughter."

The way blurred before her, and she stumbled. Instead of catching her, Patrick cushioned her fall as a gun blast shattered the night.

CHAPTER THREE

Patrick gathered up Meredith and hustled her into the trees before her father pointed his pistol at them instead of into the air. How could a father turn on his only child—his pregnant daughter—like this? Patrick should know the answer to his questions, considering his own father had left three children to fend for themselves. Not quite themselves. Grandma was there. And David.

A tree branch whacked him in the face as Meredith ducked beneath it.

David. Should he be grateful or angry that his older brother had defended him to Hughes? A man had his pride, after all. Pride that could have gotten him, or David, or Meredith, killed.

He growled, and Meredith gasped, pulling away from him. Her foot caught in the undergrowth and she tumbled to the ground. He reached for her, but she turned away, guarding her belly as if … he would strike her.

Merciful heavens. He dropped to his knees. "I won't hurt you, Meredith. Please trust me on that. Let me get you to safety."

Wherever that might be. Here beneath the trees, the light from camp and the moon faded. His breath puffed out in a frosty cloud. Meredith shivered.

Foolish! They'd die of the cold before the night was through. At least Meredith had a coat, and her flannel nightdress covered her boots, but she wore no hat. Patrick had but trousers covering his long johns, suspenders hanging at his hips, and sock feet stuffed hastily into his boots. Could he hide Meredith somewhere, then return for supplies? And food.

Without a word, she allowed him to help her to her feet. Nor did she flinch when he took her hand and led her east with as much speed as safety allowed. He heard no one following, but bullets traveled a goodly distance, and he wanted to take no risk with Meredith's life. Irony, truly. He'd worked hard to avoid responsibility, and now he had the care of a woman and her unborn child on his shoulders. How had he ended up here? And in just one day?

"Patrick? Is it safe to stop?"

Meredith's voice was small in the darkness, yet the weight of it bowed his shoulders. He couldn't be like his father and fail this task now that it was his. They needed a plan.

"We'll stop just up ahead." He led her toward a thick copse of trees near where they were harvesting. "Just up ahead."

She nodded, her breath coming in quick gasps. He'd pushed her too hard.

"Sit, Meredith." He brought a fallen log to where she stood, then helped her sink onto it before kneeling beside her. Maybe her father had overreacted and they could return to camp tonight. But what if her father still railed, and they arrived in camp only to be shot on sight? At least if Patrick left her here and went back but failed to return, the jacks would find her in the morning. If she survived.

"Why are you helping me? You risked your job and your life for me." She rubbed her belly as she searched his face, then she looked away. "Or do you plan to leave me here?"

"Leave you?" Did she read his mind?

"I won't blame you. I've already caused you more trouble than—"

"Meredith. I'm going back to camp. Alone. But not because I'm leaving you to fend for yourself. I'll set up a shelter for you for while I'm gone, but we won't survive the night without proper supplies. It's too cold. I need to go back for them, and I will return." He hoped.

"You didn't say why." She kept her gaze on the evidence of a baby growing inside of her. Another man's baby. A baby whose father had died and whose grandfather didn't care if its mother lived.

Well, Patrick wouldn't cause her to cower. Not because of him, but he wouldn't mince the truth. "Listen, Meredith. I'm doing this because it's the right thing to do. That's all."

She raised her eyes, and his gaze tangled with hers. His heart rate picked up, and he jumped to his feet.

No, no, nope. Not a chance. Yes, Meredith Hughes was beautiful, but he didn't have a death wish. Anyway, he swore he would never marry, never have children, who he would surely disappoint. Tonight was happenstance. She needed a rescue, and he was the one to provide it. That was all this was.

Agitation quickened his pace as he swept up the slash left behind from that morning. Sticks, branches, pine needles, all too green for a fire, but great for stacking into a hut of sorts. Alaric Lumber Company had lasted as long as they had because Mr. Alaric insisted on using most of the slash, like treetops, as well as replanting trees on his land, a rarity among lumber companies. However, scuttlebutt said it wouldn't be enough. Mr. Alaric already had feelers out for putting the land up for sale, but with no takers, he went ahead with this winter's harvest. There weren't many trees left, and bankruptcy was on the horizon.

What would that mean for permanent workers like the Nelsons or Hughes? For Meredith?

He laid pine boughs across the sticks he'd leaned against each other. Once again, he knelt beside Meredith, softening his voice so she didn't think his frustration was aimed at her. "Can you crawl in there? It isn't much, but it will keep you warm until I can get back."

She held up a hand as if she meant to lay it on his chest, and Patrick froze. But she didn't touch him. Instead, she curled her fingers and offered a smile. "You come back, Patrick Martins, or I'm coming to find you."

All the more reason to make sure he returned. "Wait until morning, will you?"

She rolled her eyes but dutifully crawled into the small shelter.

He peeked into the opening. "As soon as I get back, we'll head into the cutover area and build a better shelter, and a fire. I can't risk one here with all the trees. Is there anything you need me to bring you besides warmer clothes?"

"My Bible."

Her lack of hesitation took him aback, as did the request. He couldn't remember the last time he read a Bible. Sure, he went to church because Grandma made him. Even here, he went to the Sunday chapel service since David stiff-armed him. But of all the items he'd want most in Meredith's situation, a Bible never would have crossed his mind.

"It was my mother's." She pulled her coat close around her. "It's become dear to me since ... all of this."

He shifted on his heels. "You don't need to explain to me. You have nothing to prove."

Her nose bunched. Was that doubt crossing her face? A pang hit his heart. Why did he want her to think well of him? Why did it matter? Distance. Distance would help shove the unwelcome feelings back where they belonged.

"I'm going to put another limb in front of the doorway. Huddle up. I'll be back in a jiffy." After sliding a bushy branch into place, Patrick dashed away, picking up his feet so they didn't tangle with the underbrush.

Camp was quiet when he returned, the commotion over. Did that mean Hughes was asleep? Had he given up the chase? Could Patrick sneak Meredith into camp for the night? David would know.

He crept to the back of the bunkhouse where two windows allowed light into the structure. David's bunk was near the one on the north end. He tapped the secret Morse code they'd used as kids to signal one another. Before Mom died and everything fell apart.

No light blinked on. No shadow moved inside. He tapped the code again.

Then came a short tap, long tap, short tap. *R* for *Roger*. David had heard him.

Patrick stayed in the shadows as he waited for his brother's next action. Would he call him inside? Come to meet him outside? Would he have news? Patrick breathed into his bare hands, his fingertips numb. At least he'd been wearing his stocking cap when Hughes barged into the bunkhouse. He should have left it for Meredith.

"I've been worried sick," David whispered as he came around the corner of the bunkhouse.

Tension in Patrick's shoulders released. His brother would help him.

"You probably don't have a job here anymore, and we can hope Hughes won't put together that Kyle and I are connected to you once his drunken fog wears off, or we'll be out of a job too. How selfish could you be, getting involved with the foreman's daughter? Compromising—"

"Whoa." Patrick raised his palms. "I thought you'd believe me. I'm helping Meredith. I didn't cause this."

David rubbed his face.

Patrick stared at him. "You really think I would do that to a girl?"

"What was I supposed to think?" David flung out his arms. "You're in your twenties and act like an irresponsible—"

"I don't want responsibility. I'm not you."

"What are you going to do about Miss Hughes, then?"

"Make sure she's safe tonight." What else could he do? And after that, he had no idea. "Is her father sleeping it off?"

David let out a long breath, and with it his anger because his tone was entirely different when he spoke. "I suppose we should be grateful our father wasn't an angry drunk, just a sloppy one."

"He still left us." Bitterness tasted awful on his tongue.

David raised his brows, his implication clear. Their father left, but Meredith had to run from hers.

Maybe his brother had a point. "Will you help me, then?"

David hesitated.

"If for no other reason, it's Christmas. The birth of baby Jesus, and all that. Shouldn't you be more charitable to a woman in need at this time of year?"

David's face reddened in the moonlight. "For someone who hates church, you preach a convicting sermon. Yes, I will help you. It's not safe for you to bring her back here tonight. I'll get you clothes, blankets, and food. There's an abandoned cabin at the far end of the cutover land north of where we're working. I spotted it the first week we were here, when Hughes had me scout the area. It'll provide shelter for the night."

"Is it safe to light a fire there?" He couldn't believe he was asking David's opinion, but just now, with Meredith's life in danger, he needed his older brother's advice.

"As long as you make sure it's out before dawn. Then wait for me there. I'll send Kyle with information, or come myself. I'll try to clear your name and find out whether Meredith can come home."

"Even if she can stay, Meredith will remain in danger as long as she's around her father. He's not going to change overnight. Grandma would take her in, if we can get Meredith to Crow's Nest."

David looked up at the cloudless sky. "Instinct is telling me a storm is coming. My guess is two days and the road will be impassable for a while."

"Then what do we do?" Patrick dropped his voice. "What do I do?"

His brother cupped his hand around Patrick's neck. "You don't have to figure it out alone. Let's get Meredith through tonight."

Patrick nodded. David's calm assurance bolstered his confidence. He was doing the right thing.

"About your aversion to responsibility ..." David leaned in, giving Patrick no choice but to meet his gaze. "Sometimes responsibility is laid across your shoulders because of another person's actions, whether or not you're ready for it. You can choose to walk away, or shoulder the burden to care for someone else."

David meant himself when Dad walked out. He'd been in the same position as Patrick, only younger. He'd chosen to stay, just as Patrick was choosing to do with Meredith. Respect for his brother hit him, and then another emotion followed. Could he be like his brother? Did he *want* to?

"All right. Let me gather the supplies." He bumped Patrick's shoulder with his fist. "I'll meet you at the ice road in fifteen minutes."

Patrick nodded, his mind whirling. Then he remembered Meredith's one wish. Her Bible. He wasn't about to send David into Hughes's domain, risk his job and maybe his life. Patrick would handle her request himself. If he missed the rendezvous ... no. He promised he'd return to Meredith, and he would do so with her beloved Bible in hand.

Chapter Four

The cold crept into Meri's shelter. Underneath her coat. And into her soul. Why had she trusted Patrick? Would he be true to his word and return? What if her father paid him to leave her here in exchange for his job? Or his life?

What if Father kills him?

And what would happen when the jacks arrived in the morning? Her here in her nightgown and coat. She folded over her womb, holding it close as if she could hold her babe already. Her choices, her mistakes, had gotten her here.

But you're forgiven, remember?

She'd been working to memorize verses in case Father discovered Mama's Bible and took it away. She didn't want to lose so precious an heirloom, but if she had at least some of it memorized, she would always have God's Word with her. That's what Mama had said, even if Meri forgot for a while.

A shiver worked its way up her spine. As good as Patrick's shelter was, the temperature was dropping too quickly for how she was dressed. If he didn't return in the next few minutes, she needed to return to camp—if she could find her way—no matter the danger.

There she could hide near the kitchen fire until Mrs. Nelson began breakfast.

She could also find out if Patrick was doing as he promised. Then she would know whether to trust him. And if her father had hurt him, she'd ...

Another shiver shook her whole body.

Time to leave. She knocked over the branch guarding the door of her shelter and crawled into the night. An icy wind smacked her sore cheek. She was a lumberjack's daughter. She could do this. But what if Patrick returned and found her missing? He'd be frantic.

She tossed snow into her shelter, creating a writing surface, and used her finger to scrawl the word *camp*. He'd know where to find her if he came looking.

Then she set the branch-door on its side against the opening and followed the path Patrick had made when he left. Each step dampened her hope. If only she would run into Patrick returning to her. Then she'd know whether he was like every other man in her life, or if there was something different about him. She'd almost rested her hand against his chest before he left. Her concern nearly overpowered her good sense. What did she really know about Patrick Martins? He was a lumberjack, here for the winter, then gone back to Crow's Nest. He could have a wife or girlfriend for all she knew!

However, Mrs. Nelson and her husband got Patrick and his brother and friend a job here. They would have warned her about him, Mrs. Nelson especially. As the only two women in camp, they stuck together.

As the surety of that solidified, fear *for* Patrick replaced her fear *of* Patrick. She quickened her pace. Not seeing him on the road could only mean he'd run into her father. He'd already fired a gun at them once. What if he harmed Patrick because of her? All he'd done was be kind to her. Her condition was her fault. Hers and Leo's, who could no longer atone for their mistake. Patrick didn't deserve to take any blame.

A cramp in her stomach caused her to stumble. *Please let everything be okay.* She wanted this baby, no matter how it came to be. Yes, she would be ostracized, would struggle to find a job, would never marry, but she would be as good a mother as her own was to her.

The trees thinned, revealing the sleeping lumber camp. Small wisps of smoke rose from the stovepipes. No light spilled from the windows. Where was Patrick? What if he was asleep, warm in his bed, while she—no! She couldn't believe the man who'd protected her from her father would do such a thing.

Then where was he?

Another cramp and she bent double until it passed. Tugging her coat closed around her, she crept into the shadow of the men's bunkhouse. She couldn't resist peeking into the window. The moon cast a beam onto the floor inside, but no bunks were visible.

She tightened her jaw to keep her teeth from chattering. She needed better clothes before she froze.

Staying along the outside of camp, she circled around to her father's cabin. She pressed her back against the rough side and peeked around the corner. No one in sight. With quick steps, she reached the door. Slowly, she pulled it open and slipped into the darkness. Her father's snoring came from his partition. Passed out again. Good.

She tiptoed across the floor, knowing which boards creaked, until she passed through the curtain partition into her own little area. She closed her eyes and breathed a sigh of—

An arm came around her middle, and a hand covered her mouth. Her eyes widened, and she tried to fight, but this man was too strong. A lumberjack because he smelled of the woods. Pine and sap and—

"Shh. It's me, Patrick." His hold on her waist loosened. "I didn't hurt you, did I?"

She turned, freeing her mouth from his hand, but not the arm he kept around her. For some reason, she was glad. It felt safe, not threatening. "What are you doing here?"

He leaned closer. "What are *you* doing here? I told you I was getting supplies, and I promised I'd return."

She realized there was a blanket on the bed, piled with clothes, all her clothes. "You're getting me my things?" She'd assumed he'd grab a blanket for her from his own bunkhouse. What man would get her a change of clothes, especially without being asked? All she'd wanted was her Bible.

"I think I have everything, but I'm sorry I can't find your Bible. I looked everywhere I could without waking your father."

She was speechless.

"Let's get out of here. We'll go over to the mess so you can change. Then we need to meet my brother. I'm already late."

"Meet your brother?"

"He was gathering the rest of our supplies. We aren't coming back here. If we can figure out a way to get to the train, we're going to Crow's Nest. My grandmother will take you in, and you'll be safe. But if we stand here talking, we're going to wake your father."

She nodded, because what else could she do? This man had packed her belongings and planned to smuggle her to safety. Crow's Nest, that place she heard about from Mrs. Nelson. Community, friends, family. All she longed for was there. Could Patrick really help her escape? Would her father let her go?

Patrick tied the corners of the blanket together, then took her hand. She stopped him, pointed to herself. She knew the most noiseless way. He acquiesced with a wink, and the wall around her heart crumbled.

They reached the door. Freedom. She glanced back, a silent goodbye. Patrick opened the door to usher her through.

"Looking for this?" Her father's voice stopped her.

Patrick nudged her behind him. "Give her the Bible, sir, and you never have to see her again."

The strike of a match and the lantern revealed her father, holding her most prized possession. "You dare take my daughter from me?"

"I'm doing no such thing, Mr. Hughes." How did Patrick keep his voice so calm?

Meri's whole body trembled. She leaned closer to Patrick, drawing on his strength. If she aimed to begin a new life, then she needed to make a clean break of it with her father. She couldn't let Patrick fight her battle.

"You have a choice, sir," Patrick continued. "To treat your daughter better or let her go."

"How dare you!" Her father tossed the Bible to the ground and swung his fist at Patrick.

Meri squealed and ducked against the wall. Patrick blocked her father's blow but didn't return one.

"Let her go, Mr. Hughes."

Her father slammed the lantern onto the edge of the table and threw himself at Patrick. The lantern teetered, then crashed against the wooden floor, the glass chimney shattering, the kerosene spilling. Fire shot along the fuel. Patrick grunted as he took a fist to the stomach. Meri stared at the fire as it spread. She had to put it out. She had to—

"Meri!"

Patrick's shout unglued her feet. She tore the curtain from the ceiling around her bed and ran to the water bucket. Empty. Drat her father's drunkenness. She spun away from it and beat at the flames as best she could. But they latched onto the fabric, climbing toward her hands.

A thump brought her head up. Patrick and her father rolled on the floor, closer to the flames. She dodged them, tossed the burning blanket into the snow, and screamed "fire!" Then she dashed back inside. Smoke hung heavy in the air as the flames spread. She pulled down the partition encircling her father's bed. It smelled of alcohol and she tossed it aside. His bedding did as well.

"Meri, get out!" Patrick drove a shoulder into her father, his youth matched against her father's size. If Patrick could hold on, survive her father's brute force, he'd win this battle. But the fire …

Her gaze landed on her mother's Bible. She picked up her skirt and raced through the haze, snatching the book before the fire clammed it. Only now she was cornered. The fight blocking her exit, the fire closing in. She coughed into her coat sleeve and wrapped a protective arm around her belly. How could she get out now?

Shouts came from outside.

Her father landed a punch to Patrick's jaw, dropping him to the ground. With a glare at Meri, he yanked open the door and shouted, "Quick! This kid tried to burn me alive in my sleep! Nearly killed my daughter too!"

What? "No! That's not—"

Several lumberjacks pushed into the cabin.

Her father coughed. "She snuck home, and when he tried to kidnap her, he set the house on fire."

"That's not—" Her voice strangled as the smoke choked her..

"Take him to the mess and tie him up. His brother too."

No, no, no. This couldn't be happening. "Father, stop! He's—" Another cramp doubled her over. Why wouldn't anyone listen to her?

The lumberjacks attacked the flames, and someone led her out of the smoky interior. A blanket was draped over her shoulders as cold air hit her lungs. She coughed, and then another cramp caused her to cry out.

"Move aside, gentlemen. She's coming with me." Mrs. Nelson tucked her under her arm and led her away.

"Patrick." She'd gotten him into this. His brother too.

"Those Martins boys will be just fine, don't you worry. Let's make sure you and the babe are okay. Keep your mind on that right now."

Her baby. Tears stung her dry eyes. She was making a mess of everything. Her father always said she was no good. Looked like she was proving it. What hope did she have of being a mother? No man would ever marry her, not with a baby. And if she couldn't keep a lumberjack like Patrick away from her father, how was she going to protect her child?

Another cramp.

What if she caused the baby to be born too early? What if she was the reason her baby didn't survive? Mrs. Nelson had given her the basics about the months ahead of her when she'd first figured out Meri was pregnant, and this was too soon to have the baby. She had three more months at least.

"Is my baby going to be okay?" She coughed again.

"Deep breaths, dear."

"But—"

"Meredith Hughes!" Her father's voice boomed through the darkness. "Get over here and answer for what you've done."

"Let the poor girl get dressed," Mrs. Nelson shot back.

"Now!" Father snapped.

"No." Mrs. Nelson raised her chin. "Tomorrow. The girl needs to recover from what she's been through."

"Please, Father." She pressed her hand to her belly.

His gaze followed the motion. "As soon as the jacks leave in the morning, we meet in the mess hall."

"Thank you, sir," Mrs. Nelson said.

"And Meredith." Father pointed at her. "If you're not there, I'll take it out on Martins. You understand?"

She nodded. Yes, she'd be there. Because there was no way Meri was going to let one more person fall victim to her mistakes. Least of all, her baby, or the man willing to risk everything to protect her.

CHAPTER FIVE

Friday, December 19

Patrick groaned. Emyr Hughes was a beast. In every way. With fists like boulders. He rested his head against the wooden wall of the mess. He hadn't slept all night, and his stomach growled. Hughes had withheld breakfast.

Mrs. Nelson kept her distance, too, and as hungry as he was, he wouldn't want Marian's mother to suffer because of him. Responsibility. This is why he stayed away from it. It always cost someone.

Like his brother, who sat silently beside him. Eyes closed, his lanky legs stretched out, tied hands resting in his lap. As if he didn't have a care in the world. *As if.*

The door opened and Kyle slipped inside.

"The other jacks might be scared of Hughes, but they looked the other way." Kyle dropped to a knee before them, unsheathing a knife. "I managed to get all your belongings, and Meredith's, to the edge of the trees. They're ready for you to grab on your way to the train."

"Thank you. Remember to keep your head down." David turned and locked eyes with Patrick as Kyle cut the ropes around Patrick's wrists. "We're going to find a way out of this. As soon as we find Meredith."

"I'm the one who got us into this. It's my—" *responsibility.*

The corner of David's mouth turned up. "Starting to get it now?"

Yeah. Maybe.

"And I sent that message you wanted." Kyle sawed at the ropes tying David's hands. "Hughes is still in a temper, so Godspeed. I'll see you both when the ice thaws in the spring."

"Where are we going?" Patrick looked between the two. They seemed to have a plan laid out, and he was in the dark.

"We're taking Meredith to Grandma." David rubbed his wrists before Kyle gave David a hand to his feet. David held on. "This winter, think about whether being only friends with Sam is enough for you. I made room for you on my fishing crew because I want you to succeed."

Patrick stopped midway to his feet and stared at his brother. Kyle's face turned bright red.

"This situation has made me realize Adaleigh won't care how much I spend on a ring," David continued. "It's being together that matters. And now I don't want to miss our first Christmas."

Patrick hated the emotion that churned in his chest. Jealousy, longing, anger.

"Let's get going." David motioned toward the door. He and Patrick allowed Kyle to exit first so they weren't seen together.

Patrick used the opportunity to glare at his brother. "You really think Kyle is good enough for our baby sister?"

"Yes, I do." David peeked outside. "Are you ready to spring Meredith and give her a Christmas with a loving family?"

"I'm not marrying her." Preposterous. His brother had marriage on the mind.

"I said nothing of the kind." David motioned for Patrick to follow him into the cold. "Why is that word popping up in your head?"

"Because—" They circled around the corner of the mess hall.

"I know *I* want to get married. But you—how did you say it?—hate responsibility."

His brother had a point. Silence stretched between them as David led them along the back of the buildings. David had always been good at using silence as an interrogation technique, but he had grown even better at it since he met his girl. Patrick had nothing to lose voicing the question that had been nagging him all night. "What if marrying her is the only way to get her free of her father?"

David paused at the back corner of the Nelson's cabin. "Are you willing to make that sacrifice?"

"Marrying Meredith Hughes isn't a sacrifice. She's beautiful. And kind. And smart. And—" *Pregnant.*

David slipped between the Nelson's and Hughes' cabin. "You're doing more than thinking about it, brother."

Patrick growled, then remembered how Meredith had reacted to the sound in the woods yesterday. He'd scared her. "I can't.

What if I'm no better than Dad? She doesn't deserve another man mistreating her." Or her child.

David paused at the opening between the two buildings. "And why do you assume you would?"

"I'm Dad's son. I—"

"So am I."

Words died on Patrick's tongue. David was the most responsible person he knew. Irritatingly responsible. What if Patrick was more like his brother than their dad? It almost made him laugh. He resented David's oversight as much as he hated his father's actions.

"Think about it." David searched the clearing. "The camp is nearly deserted. Ready?"

Love had toned down David's workaholic tendencies. Dare he say, freed him from duty? Yet he was taking on even more. The calculation didn't compute. But his brother was happy. Ridiculously happy. And it reminded Patrick of the way David had been before Mom died. A bit mischievous, and definitely fearless. He'd always been willing to try something once. And Patrick had always been willing to follow. They made a good team. Maybe together, they'd succeed in rescuing Meredith.

He would just have to remember—David would give everything, including his life, to protect someone else. Patrick couldn't let him do that, not with a woman waiting at home for him. So if someone had to sacrifice for Meri's safety, it had better be Patrick, not his brother.

Time to step into a position Patrick had promised himself he would never shoulder. He inhaled the cold morning air. "Let's go."

Feeling like a new woman, Meri woke to bright sunshine and the Nelsons' empty cabin. Mrs. Nelson's ministrations—water, food, and rest—had worked like the best medicine.

She rubbed her belly and the baby shifted beneath. Tears blurred her vision. "That's right, little one. You and me, we'll get through this."

In no time, she traded her nightgown for the dress laid out for her. The blue cotton smelled of smoke, but appeared unharmed. Then she looked around for her Bible. Had she dropped it in the commotion last night? And what about the bundle of clothes Patrick had gathered for her? Did she have anything left to her name?

"Oh, good, you're up." Mrs. Nelson bustled into the room carrying a cup and bowl. "Eat. Drink. You have a big day ahead of you."

"Is my father sober this morning?" Meri cradled the bowl of oatmeal in her hands. Where he found his alcohol, she didn't know. It'd been illegal for years, but that hadn't stopped him.

"He seems his usual grumpy self." Mrs. Nelson laid out Meri's coat, adding a scarf, hat, and mittens that weren't Meredith's. "Eat, eat, child."

She took a bite—for the baby, because she wasn't hungry. "Why the extra winter clothes?"

"You're like a daughter to me, and mothers make sure their children are bundled against the cold." Mrs. Nelson gathered a faded quilt, hugging it to herself. "You be careful of yourself and that baby, understand?"

"What's going on?" Meri glanced around the room, hoping for clues. "Is my father ..."

Mrs. Nelson sat beside her. "I need to ask you a question, and I want you to be completely honest with me. Can you do that?"

"Yes." She drew out the word and set the bowl aside. Her stomach wouldn't tolerate another bite.

"If you could leave camp, maybe never see your father again, would you go?"

Meri jerked back. "That isn't an option."

"And that wasn't my question. If you had the ability, would you take it? Even if it meant never seeing your father again."

"It's a dream."

"Heavens, child. It's not a dream. Now, answer the question."

Meri blinked.

"You could raise your child away from your father. Be free of him. Start over. Do you want that for yourself and your baby?"

"Yes." Of course she did.

"Then are you willing to leave?"

Meri stared. "You mean this is possible?"

"All I need to know is if you want it enough to run away."

"I can't. Not alone." Nor could she leave Patrick and his brother to face her father. "No. I won't leave. Not without—"

"Mrs. Nelson, is she ready?" David Martins burst into the cabin, Patrick on his heels. Meri's mouth dropped open.

"Hey." Patrick gave her a tentative smile, then ran his gaze over her. Not like most lumberjacks did. It was almost like he was searching for ... injury. Assuring himself she was okay. As though he truly cared about her—his gaze landed on her belly—and her baby.

Mrs. Nelson rested a hand on her shoulder. "The Martins boys will get you to their grandmother's home safe and sound. I know them and they are honorable men. You will be safe with them."

For the second time that morning, her vision blurred. She quickly nodded her head. "I want to go. Please take me with you."

This was her chance at a happily ever after. Not romantically, of course. But with her baby. A new life, just the two of them.

She jumped to her feet. "Let's go before my father finds out you're gone."

David peered out the window. "Then we better hurry. We need to make it to the trees before he comes looking for us. And we need to get to the train before the snow starts."

Or they wouldn't get out until spring.

Mrs. Nelson held the coat so Meri could slip her arms inside, then wrapped the scarf around her neck while Meri secured the hat and mittens.

"You be careful, Meredith Hughes." Mrs. Nelson pulled her into a hug. "And say hi to my daughter when you arrive in Crow's Nest."

"I will, Mrs. Nelson. And thank you. For everything."

"Miss Hughes?" David was at the door.

"It's Meri. Er, Meredith." If they were traveling together, *Miss* and *Mister* would never do.

"Yes, ma'am. We need to leave."

"Kyle left a tin of food with your belongings." Mrs. Nelson walked her to the door. "There should be enough to get you to the train. I'm sorry I couldn't add more."

"Thank you, Mrs. Nelson." Patrick placed his hand on Meri's lower back, taking over from the older woman.

"Stay safe." David gave her a nod, then opened the door. "Follow me."

Patrick kept close to Meri's side as they followed David past Father's house. They ducked under the rear window in case he was inside. Then circled to the back side of the bunkhouse. The trees were one hundred feet away. The bundles of supplies should be tucked just inside. Fifty feet until freedom.

"Hey!" Father shouted. She gasped.

"Run." Patrick pushed her ahead of him. "Grab your pack and the tin and don't stop."

"Get back here, you scoundrels!" her father yelled after them.

Meri glanced over her shoulder, her mind forming a plea for him to let them go. But as she did, he pulled his pistol from a belt holster. They always carried a rifle into the woods. When had her father started wearing a gun?

He met her gaze and, instead of pointing the pistol at her, as she would have expected, he aimed at Patrick's back. He was making her choose between her baby's life and Patrick's.

"No!" she screamed.

Patrick pushed her toward his brother. "Don't look back."

David latched onto her arm. Twenty feet to the trees. Patrick ran directly behind her, protecting her, forcing her to move more quickly than she could.

Her father's heavy tread thudded behind them, hobnail boots scraping the ice-coated ground with each step. Catching up to them.

Her stomach cramped. She couldn't run as fast as the Martins brothers. She was holding them back.

"Go." She gasped for air. "Leave me behind."

"Not a chance." Patrick scooped her into his arms. Muscles used to carrying logs and tree trunks bore her easily.

"She's my daughter, Martins, and I forbid her to leave."

Then the pistol fired.

CHAPTER SIX

Patrick braced for the pain. Expected it to pierce his back. Bring him down like a hunted buck. But the pain never came. Instead, his brother dropped to the ground with a cry. Blood spread across the fabric surrounding his thigh. Patrick spun with Meri still in his arms.

"That's right, Martins." Hughes held the pistol ready to fire again. "Give me my daughter, or I aim for his heart."

"Patrick, set me down this instant." Meredith struggled in his arms. "Let me go. Take care of David."

Patrick stood in frozen indecision. Did he sacrifice Meredith or his brother? He tightened his grip on Meri.

"Father, I'm coming home," Meredith cried. "Let the Martins brothers go."

"Don't do it, Patrick." David met his gaze. "Start running. With her and the baby. Now."

The hammer cocked on Hughes's gun. Patrick had a second to decide. A life-threatening decision. He couldn't do it. He couldn't face this type of responsibility. What would he say to David's girl? Their grandmother and sister? But neither could he let Meredith and her baby face life with such a violent man.

"Last chance, Martins. Which will it be?"

And then Patrick knew that no matter what choice he made, someone would die. In fact, if he gave Meredith to Hughes, Hughes would likely kill both him and David. One look at David's face confirmed David knew that no matter what Patrick decided, he was a dead man. Patrick would lose his brother. His gut twisted.

I'm sorry, he mouthed and took his first steps toward the woods.

"Patrick, no!" Meredith sobbed on his shoulder.

Hughes swore.

And then came the crack of something hard colliding with bone. Patrick knew the sound. Rough waves had knocked over how many fishermen? The right hit on a skull and it could kill, but usually it stunned.

"Mrs. Nelson?" Meredith whispered into his neck. She no longer struggled, but held on tighter. "She hit my father with a ... frying pan."

He glanced over his shoulder to see the older woman standing over her boss, both hands gripping the handle of her frying pan. She nudged Hughes with her foot, then waved them off. "You don't have long. He'll wake shortly."

"David." Patrick hesitated. Did they leave him with Mrs. Nelson? No. Hughes could use him as leverage. There was no telling what the man would do to David once he woke up. And Mrs. Nelson? "He needs to come with us."

Mrs. Nelson glanced at Hughes. "He didn't see me, but I understand the danger. Give me a second to tend to David, and you three can find someplace safe to hole up."

Patrick set Meredith's feet on the ground. Not that he let go of her. His heart beat too hard for that. He didn't understand what he felt, only that he couldn't lose her or his brother.

She looked up at him, uncertainty clouding her usual smile. Her mouth moved, as if she attempted to form a question without words. How did this sprite of a woman make him want to be dependable?

The tear of cloth brought him back to the moment. Mrs. Nelson used fabric from her underskirt to wrap David's leg. Pain etched his brother's face, and Patrick wove his fingers between Meredith's. She squeezed, sending comfort up his arm.

He glanced at her unconscious father, who hadn't budged, then looked down at her. She stared up at him with the greenest eyes, like the pines ahead of them. He pressed his thumb to Meredith's cheek, wiping away a smudge of dirt. His willingness to sacrifice his life—his brother's life—for her told him all he needed to know about how he felt about her. The bump of her baby against his side made him pause. This wasn't a woman he could kiss and laugh off a moment later.

Meredith pressed her hand to her midsection, her cheeks reddening. Patrick cleared his throat but kept quiet. She ducked her head. "Go check on your brother."

"No need." David leaned heavily on a stick, Mrs. Nelson assuring he was steady.

"I patched him up the best I could." She cast a glance at Hughes. "He's going to wake any moment. I wish you could return to camp so I can treat it properly, but Mr. Hughes will look for you there."

Indecision encased Patrick's feet. Hughes stirred.

David placed a hand on Mrs. Nelson's arm. "Thank you for everything. Now hurry back before he realizes it was you. We'll get our things and regroup elsewhere."

She wrung her hands. "You need to get the wound cleaned out, David. It'll fester. I only stopped the bleeding."

"Go." David nudged the older woman toward camp, then limped over to Patrick and Meredith. "The snow will show our tracks, so we need to take precautions. Let's get our packs."

Patrick and Meredith followed, though Patrick searched for a reason he shouldn't do so. He always protested everything David said. But just now, he didn't have the heart for it. Instead, a newfound respect for his brother bloomed. David had been willing to give his life for them. He had a life-threatening injury, but still led them with compassion. How had Patrick missed that about David all these years? Had his resentment blinded him so solidly?

They reached the luggage Kyle stowed for them, and Patrick shouldered the majority of it. Though Meredith insisted on taking her own belongings, the fact David didn't protest told Patrick how much pain his brother was in.

They trudged through the trees, Meredith breaking the path and Patrick covering their tracks by smoothing the snow behind them by dragging a large branch behind him. The deep drifts made the going tough. Soon David's huffs became audible moans.

Patrick caught up to him. David's face was white and pinched with pain. Blood seeped through the cloth Mrs. Nelson had wrapped around his upper leg. Patrick ducked under David's arm, bearing most of his brother's weight every other step.

The overwhelming urge to cry washed over him. He hated tears. Hadn't cried since the night his mom died. Had refused to allow it of himself. Best to go through life holding everything loosely. Relationships, friendships, dreams. It could all be taken away. And if people depended on you for a thing, you had to follow through, so Patrick avoided needy people. Until now, he'd succeeded, primarily thanks to his cavalier attitude.

What if he turned out to be like his father and failed at looking after David and Meredith? At rescuing them?

Sweat broke out across his forehead. Not because of the strain of helping his brother through the snow. As one of the stronger, younger lumberjacks, Patrick had several weeks of practice lifting logs to his shoulder. And the muscle was already there from the work he did back home. Where David was the fisherman, Patrick hauled in the caught fish—something that required no responsibility, just following orders. And when his work was done, he was free to do whatever he wanted. When payday came, he didn't care how much money was in his pocket because he had no one relying on him.

Why hadn't his brother ever asked Patrick to contribute to providing for the family? He glanced at David and weaved them between two trees, avoiding the spruce trap—the hidden depression—on either side. He thought his brother overbearing, intent on making him comply. So Patrick ... didn't. Part of him knew his grandmother was not pleased, and Patrick had considered moving out. But he didn't want to be ... responsible.

Yet he left David to take care of them all on his own. No wonder David worked so much and what an absolutely worthless human being Patrick was. How much had Patrick hurt his family? By trying to avoid responsibility, had he hurt them just as much as their father did?

"I need a minute," David gasped. His breathing was rapid and shallow.

Panic clawed at Patrick. "Hey, you need to hang in there." *I need you.* A thousand tears pricked his eyes.

David squeezed his shoulder and offered a grimacing smile. "It's okay."

And then a sob hiccupped out of his chest as though he was a boy. His brother, battling pain and blood loss, was looking out for him, just as he always had since they lost their parents. Why had Patrick taken it for granted? Why hadn't he stepped up to help? Shame heated his face, and he turned away.

"Patrick." David shifted, pulling Patrick's forehead down to his shoulder, his hand strong at the back of Patrick's head. His brother would still love him. He'd seen how terrible Patrick was, been the recipient of Patrick's aversion, and still he sacrificed for him.

But Meredith ...

She stood a few feet away, witnessing this display. What must she think of him? Weak, selfish creature ... his true nature. Good thing he hadn't flirted with her. He wasn't worthy of her, and now she'd see what a despicable person he really was and would never want him near her or her child.

Meri swiped at the tear that slipped down her cheek. She'd never seen a grown man cry. Yet watching the brothers felt … wrong. As though she intruded on something sacred. She turned away.

They were nearing the cut-over field, the cabin. David needed his wound cleaned and dressed. She could do that. With all the lumber injuries over the years, she'd assisted the camp doc plenty of times. She glanced over her shoulder. Noted the perspiration on David's forehead, the whiteness around his mouth. He needed to be treated again as soon as possible.

Was her father following their tracks, though they'd tried to cover them, or had he gone back to camp? She couldn't believe Mrs. Nelson saved them, and with a frying pan! The woman must have seen Father chase after them and grabbed the closest weapon at hand.

Meri chewed her lip. Was Father all right? Surely, he'd have a massive headache after being knocked out.

"We need to keep moving." Patrick broke into her thoughts. He avoided her gaze as he situated himself under David's arm to carry his weight.

"We're almost there." This she said for David's benefit. He'd not be leaving the cabin for a while. And if the smell in the air was correct, neither would they. Snow was coming. "We've covered our trail enough. I'll keep breaking the path. You support your brother."

"Meri—"

She held up a mittened hand. "You carry enough. Let me help."

The brothers exchanged a look, then both chins sank. They wanted to be her savior. She'd never had one of those, and now she had two. Even Leo, who she'd thought would rescue her from her father, wasn't the savior she thought he was. He'd played to her emotions, her insecurities, lured her into a compromised position with the promise of marriage. And then something changed. She wasn't sure what, and now would never know, because a few days later, he'd been killed.

She dragged her feet through the snow, making the way as easy as she could for Patrick and David. David, really. Patrick had maneuvered so that David walked in the path she carved while he walked in the fresh snow beside him.

An intense desire to shield such valiant men exploded in her chest. Could she slip out after she'd doctored David's leg, find her way down the ice trail to the train by herself? As tempting as it was to lure danger away from these brothers, it might not work. Yes, her father was angry at her, and it seemed he had turned Patrick into the target because he sheltered her. But she had her unborn child to consider, too. Braving the cold and snow was not wise. And somehow, she knew Patrick wouldn't let her go alone. If she snuck out, he'd come after her.

It warmed her, that thought, as she led the way through the shin-high snow. It was tough going and her back hurt. Her abdomen still twinged, but nothing like yesterday. She pressed a hand to the child growing within her and received pressure in response. It made her think of Mary as she traveled to Bethlehem. Much further along than Meri was, of course, but still on a journey. Still feeling the movement of her unborn child. It was a marvel. And, as much as she knew her choices had been wrong, she wasn't upset at the result.

If not for her father's response, this could be a beautiful time. Why had he turned to drink? It made him such an awful man. Why was he forcing her to choose between safety and uncertainty? Society would not be kind to her, or her baby.

Her boot caught on an unseen root. She dropped to her knees, careful to catch her fall so she didn't land on her belly.

"Meri!" Patrick was by her side, lifting her out of the snow. "Are you all right?"

David leaned on his stick, watching.

She dusted herself off. "I'm fine."

"Just getting tired." Patrick raised a hand, and reflexively, she ducked away. He grimaced. "We'll get you to the cabin. Don't worry."

No doubt of that. Looking past the brothers, she scanned the trees for signs of her father. All was quiet. The scent of pine strong. Good thing Mr. Alaric insisted on planting new trees in place of the ones they'd cut down. How sad it would be to lose all the forests in the search for lumber.

Just the same, her heart squeezed a few moments later. Like a tree graveyard, the cutover field stretched before them, all stumps and slash. On the far side stood the cabin, bare in the desolate place. The pristine white of the snow made it appear dirty and broken.

"Wait." Patrick halted her. "Let me make sure your father hasn't beaten us here."

"You think he means to cut us off?" David spoke matter-of-factly.

Patrick met his brother's gaze. "I can't risk your lives on assumptions. I'm going ahead, and if the cabin is safe, I'll come back for you."

"But what if he's there? What if he ambushes you?" Her heart pounded at the thought of losing him. He'd protected her instead of sending her away in disgrace. She reached for his arm. "Let's stay together. Please."

His jaw worked. "It's not the responsible thing to do."

David grasped his other shoulder. "But we get a choice and we choose you."

CHAPTER SEVEN

Patrick, with David leaning on his shoulder, led the way across the cutover field. Why Meredith and David insisted on going with him to the cabin instead of waiting in safety, he didn't understand. The one time he was willing to bear a burden, and no one took him up on it. Did they not think him capable? Hughes may have been knocked unconscious, but once he regained his wits, he'd be madder than a bear.

Patrick pushed the doubt away as they neared the old structure. Logs were saddle-notched together, but in between, the chinking had mostly washed away, leaving the interior vulnerable to critters and the elements. David leaned against the cabin, as ashen as the clouds hiding the sun. Meredith rubbed her belly, lines etched into her face. Emotion welled. He wanted to care for her, protect her, but that included her baby and that thought scared him.

No. Right now the best way he could help everyone was by making sure the cabin was safe.

Patrick borrowed David's stick, lifted the latch, and eased open the door.

He pressed his nose into the crook of his elbow as the overwhelming smell of fermented grain churned his stomach. His father had smelled this way too many times to count. He couldn't let it stop him, however. Meredith and David needed shelter.

He pushed inside, letting in the gray light. There, in the center of the one-room cabin, sat a still. A mouse skittered across the floor, leaving behind the fallen barley stalk it'd been nibbling on. Even though it was the only living creature here, was it safe to stay? The making and sale of alcohol was illegal. And then, the sight of another item in the room made his stomach drop.

The old coat in the corner. He'd seen it many times, and it further confirmed the fact they couldn't stay here any longer than necessary. For he knew who used this cabin. Patrick returned outside, determined to get David patched up enough to leave as soon as possible.

Only, when he exited the cabin, a snowflake landed on his cheek. He looked up, and another flake caused him to blink. The snow had arrived, and if David was right about this storm—and as experienced a fisherman as he was, he was almost always right—their chance of escape had disappeared.

Meri felt the first snowflake before she saw the second. A smile lifted the corner of her mouth despite ... well, everything. How could she not smile at the dot of perfection that melted as it landed on her mitten?

And then reality slammed into her. The snowstorm David had predicted. The one Mr. Alaric had telegraphed her father about the other day. It had hit his home in Minnesota hard, and he wanted his lumber camp to be prepared. In all likelihood, they would be snowed in with no way to get the lumber to the train until they cleared and watered the ice road.

It also meant she, Patrick, and David had a slim chance to even make the train, if it hadn't already departed for safety by the time they arrived. She glanced at David, who had sunk to the base of the cabin's outside wall, eyes closed, head resting on his upraised knee. His bad leg stretched out, the red stain soaking through the bandage. He needed treatment immediately. Making the train was out of the question.

Patrick returned, jaw set.

"What is it?" David used a single breath to voice the question, clearly barely holding on.

"We can't stay here." Patrick leaned the stick beside his brother. "If I work quickly, I can build us a shelter for the night. We'll—"

"No." Meri stepped between the brothers, facing Patrick so she could communicate her urgency without David noticing. "That wound needs attending now. We stay here until he's ... okay."

Patrick pulled his stocking cap from his head, defeat rounding his shoulders.

Meri advanced until she stood toe-to-toe with him. "You're doing exactly what needs to be done. And now you'll do it again. Let's get David into the cabin and—"

"That's just it." Patrick grabbed her arms. "This is an illegal still."

"You think a policeman will happen upon us in the middle of a storm?"

"This is where your father gets his alcohol."

"How—" Meri sagged. How else would he get it?

Patrick rubbed his hands over her coat sleeves. "I think it's owned by your father."

Meri pulled away. "Why would he do that? He has a great job. He has no need—"

"There's a spare coat hanging on the wall. It's his, Meri. I've seen him wear it."

Meri shook her head, not wanting to believe it.

"And if this is your father's still, it means he'll find us, whether he knows to look for us here or not. We can't stay."

Meri looked over at David. "We have no choice, Patrick. Your brother needs help, and the snow is only going to get worse."

His gaze roved the cutover landscape around them. She could almost see the wheels turning in his head.

"Patrick?" She rested a palm on his chest, the heavy coat muffling the pounding of his heart. He met her eyes. Warmth spread through her, giving her the courage to say, "You can do this. I trust you."

Then she reached up and placed a kiss on his scruffy cheek.

Several hours later, night having descended, Patrick could finally revisit the kiss Meri had given him. He stood outside the cabin, his hand resting on the place where her lips had touched his cheek. Such a chaste, gentle kiss, but for all its simplicity, it had been a monumental gift. And it had touched him ... deeply.

He paused before returning inside after visiting the outhouse. Snow fell in sheets, obscuring the cutover field and the forest beyond. The wind attempted to tuck snow under his coat. Then, when he turned up his collar, it smacked him in the face. Hopefully, it would also keep Hughes in camp, because they'd never see or hear him coming in this storm.

Both Meri and David slept inside. David's wound had been bleeding again, and he'd passed out as Patrick dragged him inside, a blessing for the pain Meri put him through next. Meri had directed Patrick lay David on the floor under a window where she could see the wound better. She'd cleaned it using moonshine Patrick found in one of the jugs in the kitchen area. The wound was deep, what looked like a chunk taken from David's leg, but not as bad as it could have been had the bullet pierced all the way through his thigh or lodged inside. Meri was able to get the ugly slash bandaged, but the effort had exhausted the last of her strength, and she'd laid down on the cot to rest.

The cabin, for all of its illegal contents, had the amenities they needed to survive the next day or two. Plenty of dried wood for the fireplace. A working water pump. Canned food in the pantry. Not much else, but they didn't need anything else. Meri could have the cot with its threadbare blanket. David still lay unconscious under the window. And Patrick would keep watch.

The responsibility he'd artfully avoided for years had caught him unawares. It swirled around him like the wind, pressing in and threatening to undo him if he stepped out of line. And it wasn't just any responsibility, like putting food on the table or seeing a girl home after a date. No, he had three lives completely dependent on him and danger bearing down in multiple forms.

This spring, he'd survived a tornado by lying in a ditch. It had been thrilling. Dangerous. Foolish. Not that he'd cared. He'd returned home expecting to taunt his brother with his exploit, to needle his grandmother that he'd survived without her interference. Only, his little sister had been injured in the storm, and his brother had nearly lost his life. It had been jarring to learn, and so he'd tucked his own experience away.

Now his brother was facing death again, this time because of Patrick's choices. Not only his, of course. Had Patrick allowed Meri to face her father on her own, David wouldn't be caught in the middle. Yet even now, he wouldn't change what he'd done, and he knew David wouldn't either. His brother was a hero. As for himself ...

Patrick bowed his head, partially in deference to the icy wind, partially in prayer. He was out of practice, but after the last couple days, after the trust Meri and David placed in him, it pulled him back to his mother's God, something not even that tornado had been able to do. If he didn't want to be like his father, and fail in the duty laid upon his shoulders, then he needed help. God's help.

Snow cut his cheeks, but somehow, the lash of snow felt necessary. As though it purged his inner turmoil. He crossed his arms and blinked as his vision blurred. His mother had loved Christmas. *I feel closest to God at Christmastime,* she'd always said, *because the babe born in the manger was called Immanuel, God with Us.* Surely, God had been with his mom. She was an angel, especially to a little boy like him. And when she was gone, the devil took her place in the face of his father. Drunken, despairing. Then he left.

Patrick sniffed, but it didn't stop a tear from escaping and freezing on his cheek. The anger and hurt of the little boy inside swirled like the storm. He swore he would never be like his worthless father, but how was he any better? A man who avoided responsibility like a child? He might not fail those around him, but that was because he never allowed anyone to trust him, to think well enough of him to be disappointed. Yet he did let down his grandmother, his brother and sister. For all his efforts, he still hurt those closest to him. And that was shameful.

Would God be with the likes of him? He didn't deserve it, no doubt about it. However, for Meri and David, surely God would intervene. Another of his mother's sayings echoed in the wind. Or was it a Bible verse? *It was good to make merry, for this one was lost, and now is found.* Well, he felt as lost as ever.

With less than a week until Christmas, and a woman with child under his care, he couldn't help but make a connection to the baby whose birth was celebrated at this time of year. How had Joseph felt, taking Mary to Bethlehem? Mary, who expected a baby who wasn't Joseph's? How had he felt when he received the warning to flee to Egypt lest the king kill Mary's son? A story Patrick had forgotten until now.

Meri wasn't Patrick's wife and her baby wasn't his, yet the protective emotion he felt for them overwhelmed him. Cold, danger—it didn't matter. He'd do anything to keep them safe. The realization hit him like a gust from the blizzard. And he didn't understand why. How had Meri come to mean so much to him in the weeks he'd spent watching her from afar and the couple of days he'd spent in her presence?

Her father. That had to be it. Not some misplaced attraction.

Ever since his own father had turned to drink, he could spot a drunk in an instant. He'd pegged Hughes from the first day, and had it not been for Mr. and Mrs. Nelson getting David, Kyle, and him the job, he would have walked away. He didn't need a foreman like that. And Meri didn't deserve a father like that.

A shiver convulsed his body—both from the weather and the emotion. Time go inside before he froze. He pulled open the cabin door, wrestling it shut behind him. Meri and David slept through the blast of icy wind that had followed him inside.

Patrick unwrapped his outwear, left his snowy boots by the door. Wished he could leave his thoughts there, too. He wasn't settled in his soul, but if he didn't come to terms with his own struggle, he wouldn't do Meri and David any good. Patrick grabbed a stick to stoke the fire. He just didn't know how to overcome his past. How to not be so ... lost.

CHAPTER EIGHT

Saturday, December 20

Meri woke feeling sore, yet warm. She stretched, then pushed to a sitting position. The cabin was dark except for the glow from the fireplace. Someone had kindled it. David's form rested under the window where they'd left him, but Patrick was absent.

She rubbed her belly, then stood. Every muscle ached, and her clothing smelled like the stale blanket that had been on the cot. Why hadn't she realized her father's absences meant he harbored a secret? She'd assumed he had camp business. It had never occurred to her that he operated a still, of all things.

She laid the back of her hand against David's forehead, then his neck. No fever. Good. But he didn't stir when she touched him. She needed to get a look at that leg again. Patrick said David had a girl waiting back home. They both had a grandmother and a sister. Three women who would be missing them this Christmas. And if these two men were killed because of Meri? How could she live with herself?

She donned her coat and finding a kettle in the rudimentary kitchen, she took it to fill on her way to the outhouse, only to be pushed back by the snow and wind and cold as she opened the door.

"Meri!" Patrick appeared from the gray outside and grabbed the door edge, then her arm, his body blocking the storm from entering the cabin.

She flinched, and he released her. Dismay at her ingrained reaction swamped her. She liked the feeling of his hand on her arm. Once she knew it was coming. She raised her gaze and the kettle. "I want to heat water over the fire and—" Her cheeks warmed at the mention of her personal needs, which were growing more urgent by the moment.

"Come on. I'll take care of this as I walk you there." He tucked her under his arm, sheltering her on the way to the outhouse.

This sense of security was such a new feeling to her. Over the years, she had learned to discern which lumberjacks were safe to allow close and those who weren't. Those she could easily flirt with and those who would expect more because of it. Then came Leo—and his promises of protection from her father—and the baby. She pressed a hand to her abdomen, and the child squirmed beneath her touch.

Had she loved Leo or the possibility of escape? Would he have compromised her in her moment of weakness if he loved her? She'd gone to him after her father came home one evening, drunk and taking his anger out on her. She had feared he'd hurt her worse than leaving the usual bruises, and she'd run to Leo, her fiancé. In her distraught state, she'd had no will to fight his advances. His words of endearment were so opposite the hate spewed from her father. They were to be married soon, he assured her. They'd go west together when the company folded because of the stock market crash.

And then, three days later, he was dead. A rope brace had broken while he was cutting down a widowmaker, and he'd plummeted to the forest floor. An accident, her father told her. Part of the danger of being a lumberjack.

Patrick led her back inside and Meri scurried away from the cold. After they removed their hats, coats, and boots, Patrick handed her the kettle, packed with snow. His eyes smiled at her, but his face was wind-chapped and his clothes and beard packed with snow. How long had he been outside before she interrupted him?

She spun away, her emotions jagged. She poked the fire and rested the kettle on the grate above it. Could she trust this feeling she had about Patrick? And if she did, what did that mean?

Her reputation was in tatters, she had no home to speak of, and in a few months, she'd have a baby. She'd be an unwed mother. There was no bright future for her, especially because she had no desire to give up her baby. She wanted a family. But in her condition, no other man would have her. This baby was all she had. Even if her father did welcome her back, she would never live under his roof again. Not after what he'd done the past couple days. And, despite the way Patrick looked at her, with a tenderness she couldn't quite remember seeing in Leo, she couldn't saddle him with a woman like herself and a baby that wasn't his.

It was good his brother was here, even if he was unconscious. It kept Patrick's reputation intact because she had no doubt he would do the honorable thing concerning her if anyone called into question their time together.

As it was, he protected her from her father's insinuations at great cost.

She watched the snow turn into water. Listened to Patrick shuffle around the cabin behind her. Let the warmth of the fire seep past her defenses. For now, she'd relish the sense of home she had with the Martins brothers, even in a place such as this. The way the snow and wind encircled them like an icy moat—for surely, her father wouldn't chase them in this storm. And when the storm had passed and reality arrived, she'd face the future.

Until then, she'd count these hours as her own special Christmas gift. She'd worry about tomorrow when it came.

"How's the leg?" Patrick crossed his arms as he knelt beside his brother, who was finally awake. It had been hours of snow buffeting the cabin outside and him pacing inside. Meri had discovered David's wound showed signs of infection that morning, and a fever followed.

"Still feels like fire." David blinked up at him, eyes glassy.

"You need to drink this." Meri bustled over with a tin cup. "Patrick, help him sit up."

Patrick flexed his jaw. Emotion tangled in his chest. The storm kept them safe but also kept them from getting the medical care David needed. At least they had Meri. After their morning visit to the outhouse, she'd discovered some garlic and honey in the cellar below the kitchen and made some sort of compress. She also continued to clean the wound with snow water she first boiled, then cooled. Frankly, he wouldn't know what to do for David without her.

"Patrick." Meri's voice stirred him to action. He slid his arm under David's shoulder and leveraged him to a forty-five degree angle. David moaned, but Meri had the cup at his lips, forcing him to swallow.

"He's so warm." Patrick's heart rate climbed, worry choking him. *Responsible. You're responsible.* The words repeated every time he felt the heat from David's body.

"I know." Meri glanced at Patrick, but focused on getting David to drink the entire cup of whatever she was giving him. "That means there's infection. I need to keep cleaning the wound and doing what I can."

Having finished the water, David groaned as Patrick laid him down.

"Rest is healing." Meri patted David's shoulder, then returned to the fire.

"You care for her." David's whisper hung between them.

Patrick had no answer. Everything inside felt foreign and confusing.

"Patrick." David squeezed Patrick's hand, which he still held. "Do me a favor?"

Patrick opened his mouth, then snapped it closed. Could he fulfill a favor? What if he failed? What if … He froze, unable to turn left or right.

"If I don't make it—"

"Stop." Boyish tears burned his eyes. "You're going to make it home. You're in this mess because of me."

"No. We're in this mess because of Emyr Hughes." David struggled to prop himself up on his elbow, grabbing Patrick's shoulder with his free hand. "Listen to me. Brothers stand by one another. I wouldn't have left you to face the man alone. Do you understand that?"

"I don't deserve it." He looked up at the ceiling, feeling all of ten, the pain of essentially losing both father and mother fresh as if it happened yesterday.

"Look at me, Patrick." David shook his shoulder. "Me being here has nothing to do with whether you deserve it or not. We're brothers. That's all I require to stand beside you. Do you hear me? I love you. We're family."

Patrick's chin wobbled. He couldn't break down in front of David. Or Meri. He tore away from his brother's hold, grabbed his outerwear, and pushed into the blizzard before having his coat fully buttoned.

We're brothers. That's all I require.

Is that all God required of him too? To be a son? That story, of the son returning home to be welcomed by his father. The father wanted nothing from him, for the man was already his son, and he loved him. Patrick didn't have an earthly father like that, but he had a brother. A brother who loved him unconditionally, exactly the way their mother said God loved him.

The realization had him leaning against the side of the cabin as the wind, ice, and snow buffeted him. If he stepped away, he'd be lost in the whiteness. Yet, in that moment, he'd never felt more found.

Meri swiped a tear as she stirred canned beans in a pot over the fire. The cabin was too small for her to not have heard the conversation between the brothers. Since she'd learned she was expecting a child of her own, not only had her tears become more frequent, the concept of God's love had become more real to her. God loved her like she loved her baby. God loved Patrick that way too.

And David thought Patrick might care for her?

Another tear slipped down her cheek. As sweet as that was, she couldn't encourage it. She refused to saddle a protector like Patrick with her situation. Not to mention, she was the reason his brother battled a fever. She was doing her best to keep the wound clean with the resources she had, but the way it festered made her stomach clench. If he lost the leg—or worse—because of her …

She shuddered. No, nothing could ever develop between her and Patrick.

Speaking of the man, he blew back into the cabin along with a shovelful of snow. "It smells good in here."

Her heart stumbled. It was such a homey thing to say. And then she met his gaze. It forced her back a step. He was different. Changed.

The man who'd left a quarter of an hour ago was not the one who returned in time for an early supper. She'd thought the turmoil in his eyes was for her situation, for his brother, but the storm had cleared from his face. Nothing had changed, yet he was at peace.

However, it was the concern she'd seen in his eyes that allowed her to trust him in the first place. Now doubts flooded her as if the packed dirt below her feet had turned to water.

"Hey, what's wrong?" He took several steps toward her, arm outstretched.

Oh, why was this cabin so small? She spun away from him, putting the table between them to check on David. The poor man slept now, having exhausted himself talking to Patrick.

"Meri." Patrick stayed on his side of the cabin.

Her heart pounded. He'd called her *Meri*. But the only reason he could be at peace was because he'd put his priorities in perspective. Right? Of course, his brother came first—the way it should be. He would leave her here as soon as the storm ended. He'd get help for David, even if that meant leaving her to face her fate alone. It was the right thing to do. That's why Patrick was at peace. He'd made his decision.

"Meri, your beans are burning."

Meri again. *Why?*

He silently gave her room to dish up the meal. The howling of the wind lessened. That meant time was short. She set his bowl on the table, then stepped toward David, intending to wake him to help him eat.

"Sit and eat, Meri. I'll feed him." Patrick touched her shoulder, and she jerked away.

Meri, Meri. Even her father didn't call her by her nickname. This time, her tears came. She was so confused. She swiped at her eyes.

"Oh, Meri." Patrick hovered both hands a breath away from her upper arms, as if he wanted to hold her but wouldn't without her permission.

The tears came harder. "You're such a good man."

He was shaking his head.

But she nodded. "You and your brother don't deserve anything that has happened to you. It's my fault, and I'm releasing you of your responsibility."

He jerked as if she slapped him. "What if I don't want to be released?"

"What?"

This time, he raised a palm to her face. She squeezed her eyes closed, waiting for the contact. When it came, it was feather-light ... and warm. His thumb swiped at her tears. "I want the responsibility, Meri. All of it."

She opened her eyes to find his gaze on her. His brother was right—he cared about her. Her breath hitched. This wasn't a look she remembered seeing in Leo's eyes. The father of her child hadn't cared about her the way this man did.

"I hate that touch scares you." His voice roughened.

His gaze dipped to her belly, his free hand rising. Pausing. She grasped it and rested it where she'd last felt the baby move. A heartbeat later, Patrick gasped. His eyes found hers, wonder eclipsing all other emotion. Her cheeks heated, but she couldn't stop the shy smile that lifted her lips. To share this moment with him.

His thumb raised her chin. His gaze dropped to her lips, then back to her eyes. A question there. Did she want him to kiss her? She lifted to her toes, and Patrick met her in the sweetest kiss she'd ever experienced. Gentle and caring. He pulled away after a moment, not asking for more, not pressuring her. Instead, the hand that held her cheek slipped around her shoulders and tugged her into a hug. For all its awkwardness because of her belly, she never wanted to leave that circle of safety.

"Listen," Patrick whispered.

"The wind died down." Her pulse kicked up for a whole different reason.

Patrick tightened his hold. "I'll make a travois, and we'll take David—"

"We?"

"Of course. I'm not leaving you here. We need to get you to safety as soon as possible. If the storm is stopping, it means your father could be on his way."

CHAPTER NINE

Sunday, December 21

Night stretched on forever, while the storm blew itself quiet. Patrick stayed awake, making the travois and keeping watch. His muscles ached from the tension, from praying the snow would fall until morning to keep Emyr Hughes from looking for them before they could escape.

He peered out the window, the first haze of daylight sparkling off the glittering snow. It was time to leave.

Meri lay on the cot before the fire, and he rested a gentle hand on her small shoulder. He'd allowed the fire to die out and already the chill crept through the room.

Meri opened her eyes, met his gaze. She gave a single nod. She was ready to face the day.

Patrick left her to get ready and woke his brother. "We need to get you on your feet."

David shivered. "Leave me here. I'll send Hughes on a goose chase."

"No. Hughes would kill you, same as he would have if we'd left you at the camp." Patrick tucked his arm under David's shoulders and lifted. "I've hauled logs heavier than you. Let's go."

"Where are we going?" Meri opened the door, and a gust of fine snow blew into their faces. Good. The wind might cover some of their tracks.

Patrick had considered leaving while there was still snow falling, but he couldn't risk losing their way in the dark, not when David and Meri depended on him. The weight of it lay heavy on his shoulders, but he'd chosen this mantle. He wouldn't fail like his father.

David squeezed his shoulder as if he heard Patrick's inner thoughts. It bolstered him, knowing his brother believed in him. He laid David on the sled he had created, bundled all the dirty blankets they'd found in the cabin around him, then took up the two poles he'd use to pull his brother.

"Patrick." Meri stopped in front of him, hands on her hips, her breath frosty in the rapidly lightening dawn. "Where are we going?"

This was the part he'd debated all night. David needed a doctor and Meri needed to get as far away from camp, and her father, as she could. That part was simple. As was the fact that both situations would be solved by following the ice road to the town of Manitowish Waters. The road would be empty. It being Sunday, the camp would remain quiet, the lumberjacks sleeping the day away. And therein lay the trouble. It allowed Hughes freedom to look for them and they'd be open targets on the road.

He took a step, the sled following despite his brother's weight. Only, it brought him that much closer to Meri, and she wasn't getting out of his way. It made the corner of his mouth turn up. This woman who had been tentative to his touch as recent as last night now blocked his way. He liked it. Liked seeing her trust him enough to stand up to him.

He shook his head. Now was not the time for that. "We have to follow the ice road to town. I see no other options. We have to get you away from camp and David to a doctor." He glanced at the bump that was barely concealed within her coat, then at her shoes. "Can you walk that far?"

She raised her chin. "For my baby's life, for yours and David's, I'll do anything."

Meri stopped and rubbed her belly. The sun was fully up, betraying their slow pace. Without the proper boots, she was forced to walk beside the ice road rather than on it. Patrick had gotten her two sticks to help her walk in the deep snow that covered the uneven ground. The ache she'd felt before they had to run from her father was back.

She glanced over her shoulder. While Patrick's hobnail books gave him traction on the snow-covered ice beside her, he struggled through the drifts that had blown over the road. The determined set of his jaw encouraged her on.

Lifting her knees high, she started forward again. Once they got to Manitowish Waters, what would happen? They would take David to the doctor, but then what? Where would she stay? Or go?

Perhaps we'll move to Crow's Nest.

Mrs. Nelson's words from the other day came back to her—was Mrs. Nelson okay? And what if Meri could move to Crow's Nest, too? Would Patrick help her get there?

Boom!

Meri screamed as the sound of a gunshot sent birds scattering into the air.

"Meri down. Get down." Patrick pulled her into the snow. Someone had followed them, was shooting at them! She spun to Patrick, her panic making her unable to think of a plan. He would know what to do.

His eyes darted around them. The wind had covered his tracks along the ice road, but not hers alongside. They were clear and deep. Men's voices grew closer. Had her father brought reinforcements? There was nowhere to run.

"Shh." Patrick drew her into the circle of his arms and crouched down with her beside the travois, his body between her and the gunman. David shifted on the travois, and Patrick laid a hand on his shoulder. Meri's heart pounded in her chest. The baby kicked at her ribs.

Out of the shadows, two men loomed.

Her father glared at her. The second man, Junior Aleric, Mr. Aleric's son—what was he doing here?—smirked at her. "You know, Hughes, Kingsman never had these problems. Now get this road cleared for the shipment."

Meri gasped. Kingsman? Leo Kingsman? Her Leo? And a shipment? Not lumber because the camp rested on Sundays. *Moonshine.* Leo was part of her father's operation.

No, Junior's operation.

Patrick leapt to his feet. Pain twisted Meri's middle. This wasn't happening. If Leo had been working with Father and Junior, then could Patrick betray her too?

Patrick stood wide, placing himself between danger and Meri and David, waiting for the inevitable. Whether taking the ice road had been a good plan or not, the execution had failed.

Poor word choice, that. His execution might very well occur within the next few minutes. Hughes had shot David, after all. What would stop him from finishing the job here and now? Patrick had no way to protect Meri or David, except with his life. And when he was gone, what good would that do for any of them? This is why he'd avoided responsibility all these years. Just like his father, he couldn't be trusted.

"Martins." Emyr Hughes pointed the pistol at him, his hand the steady one of a sober man. He stood beside a man Patrick remembered seeing in camp once before. Alaric's son. A man who came to give orders without understanding the work.

"What are you waiting for?" The stranger crossed his arms, stretching the seams of his fur-collared, double-breasted coat. "If you can't shoot him, Just make one of them marry her like Kingsman planned to do. You wanted to keep it all in the family."

The snake!

Meri whimpered from where she remained crouched in the snow behind Patrick. The sound ripped something inside of him. His own soul had made such a sound at one time. It was the pain of betrayal. That Meri would experience it ... and without the support Patrick had, the family he had taken for granted. But she had support—she had him. He wouldn't leave her alone, just as his family had persistently stayed beside him, no matter how hard he'd pushed them away. He'd fight for Meri. Like David fought for him.

Patrick closed his fists to keep hold of his emotion as he confronted her father. "Leo Kingsman planned to marry your daughter because you made him?"

"He was willing enough." Hughes waved his hand. "Until the end. Then he wanted out of the business, so I ended him."

"You what?" Meri struggled to her feet. Patrick slipped a hand under her elbow to help her up the embankment and onto the road.

"He—" Hughes stopped as his gaze fell to Meri's unborn child and filled with rage. His voice shook as he said, "Why didn't I see it before? He did that to you, didn't he?"

Tears dripped down Meri's cheeks. "I thought he loved me, and when you were so angry with me, we planned to run away together. But he did it to spite you, didn't he?"

If Leo hadn't already died, Patrick would have shown him just what he thought of such behavior.

Junior snorted. "Kingsman had more of a backbone than I thought. Good for him. I'm sorry we had to lose him. Now, what do we do with all of you? Obviously, you know too much about our operation, so either you join us and we say we found you after you were lost in the blizzard, or we find a way to get rid of you for good."

Meri's breath caught, and Patrick tightened his fingers on her elbow. He wouldn't let it come to that. He hoped.

"My daughter was never meant to be a pawn." Hughes's face turned purple. "I agreed to get rid of Kingsman because he wouldn't be good for my daughter. I was willing to end these brothers because I thought they'd ruined her. Everything I've done has been to give her the best life I could. I promised my wife that. Our daughter would be a real lady someday. It was the least I could do after she died."

"You ..." Meri's voice faltered.

Patrick gaped at the man. "You beat your daughter." Whether or not that was what Meri had meant to say, it was the truth. "How is that doing the best you could?"

"Who cares?" Junior pulled out a gun. "I'm gonna recommend my father close the camp immediately. In the meantime, let's put all of you out of your misery. Truly. This is pitiful."

"No. I am the only man allowed to lay a hand on my daughter." Hughes roared and swung his pistol at Junior. The younger man's eyes went wide as Hughes pulled the trigger.

Patrick tucked Meri's face into his chest and crouched with her again, shielding her as best he could. She sobbed into his chest as he watched Hughes stand over Junior. Would the next bullet be for Patrick?

"Drop your weapon!" a new voice shouted. He would know that man's voice anywhere. He'd heard it often enough, and with that commanding tone too.

Meri trembled. "Who is that?"

"My uncle." How had the old detective gotten here? And with a companion? "I don't know who he brought with him."

The man wore a knit cap over brown hair and a thick jacket. It rode up on the bottom as he approached Hughes and Patrick caught the shine of a sheriff's badge.

"You kids okay?" Uncle Mike's mustache bobbed as he studied them. Patrick's words failed, so he nodded. Junior needed medical attention more urgently than they did. His uncle seemed to understand because he knelt beside Junior. "He's gone."

"Mr. Hughes, you are under arrest for murder." The sheriff took possession of Hughes's pistol.

"You take care of her." Hughes looked directly at Patrick as the sheriff pushed Hughes to his knees. "Don't you betray her like Kingsman. You be better to her than I ever could be, y'hear?"

Patrick tucked his chin to catch a glimpse of Meri's face. It was white as the snow, but still so beautiful. Patrick met Hughes's stare. "That is why I couldn't let you lay another hand on her. Even if it cost me everything."

Meri shuddered. Her arms wrapped around her stomach.

"Your scene, Yarwood." Uncle Mike spoke to the sheriff.

"Stay here." Yarwood secured Hughes' wrists. "I'll take this one back to Manitowish Waters and send my deputy with the coroner."

The two law enforcement officers discussed a few more details, but Patrick ignored them, more concerned about Meri and David. His brother's face was scrunched in pain, but he gave the slightest of nods. Approval. It ignited a thought that would have been the furthest possible idea to ever have entered Patrick's mind not many days ago—and he'd be torn apart if Meri said no.

CHAPTER TEN

"There you are!" A woman with a brown braid partially covered by a stocking cap stopped a sleigh driven by two huge draft horses beside them. Did Patrick have a girl?

Despite the doubt, gratefulness washed over Meri as pain twisted her middle. She leaned on the walking sticks Patrick had retrieved for her. They couldn't get to town fast enough. Sheriff Yarwood had walked ahead with her father, instructing them to wait with Detective O'Connor for the sleigh.

"Am I glad to see you." Patrick held the horses as the woman jumped down. "Though how you and Uncle Mike have such exceptional timing, I'd like to know."

"Kyle sent your uncle and me a telegram at David's request. Said you were in trouble. I wasn't about to let your uncle come here alone, was I? Of course Yarwood made me wait with the sled when we heard a gunshot." The woman brushed past them, dropping to her knees beside the travois, her hand going to David's face. "He's feverish."

"Adaleigh, first let me introduce you to Meredith Hughes. Meri, this is David's girl, Adaleigh Sirland." Patrick lifted the handles of the travois and started toward the back of the sleigh, forcing Meri and Adaleigh to keep moving. "Meri treated the wound as best she could with the few resources we had. We need the doc."

Adaleigh glanced around Patrick. "It's a pleasure to meet you, Miss Hughes. Thank you for doing everything you did for David."

Her gaze lowered to Meri's stomach, and Meri wrapped her arms around her unborn baby.

"How long have you been on your feet?" Adaleigh skirted Patrick to walk alongside Meri. She even tucked her arm in hers, heedless of the walking stick. Would she do that if she knew Meri didn't have a husband?

Wait. Adaleigh had called her *Miss Hughes*. "You know?"

Adaleigh shrugged. "Easy enough to piece together when the sheriff told us who you were and then seeing you now. How are you feeling?"

Meri gaped at Adaleigh, trying to wrap her mind around the woman's reaction. No judgment, only concern. That wasn't what she'd receive anywhere else, but it seemed that when it came to the Martins family, she could trust them to accept her just as she was.

"Sheriff Yarwood set us up at a small inn. You can stay with me. I know nothing about these things, but I can see on your face you need rest." Then Adaleigh lowered her voice. "And if you need to talk ..."

Meri whipped her head around and saw empathy in this stranger's eyes. Meri's heart stuttered. This woman had a story that gave her the ability to relate to Meri's experience. Meri shouldn't pry—she wouldn't want someone to pry into *her* life—but suddenly, she wanted to know everything about Adaleigh. And maybe tell Adaleigh her own story too.

Wednesday, December 24

Patrick read David's Bible as he sat beside his brother's bed, finding new meaning in the words. They occupied a small room in the Manitowish Waters Inn. Evening had fallen, and all was quiet around them, but nervous energy pulsed through him.

Three days had seen remarkable recovery in his brother. Sheriff Casper Yarwood oversaw the case against Emyr Hughes and the burial of Junior Aleric. He also halted work until details were worked out regarding Mr. Aleric—including the establishment of the man's innocence in the illegal creation and sale of alcohol—and the appointing of a new foreman should the company continue. Rumor had it Mr. Nelson was in the running, but it required leaving Wisconsin after this winter, since Aleric had no choice but to move his business west if he was cleared and wanted his company to survive.

David stirred on the bed. "I can't believe I've napped again. I can't remember the last time I slept this much."

"You needed it, brother." Patrick glanced to where David's legs were covered by the blanket. The doctor said he'd served in the Great

War, had amputated many a leg better off than David's, and swore he'd save as many as he could if he made it home. David's was one of those.

"And you?" David struggled to sit up, and Patrick reached to help. "You haven't slept much, judging from those shadows below your eyes. Have you talked to Meredith?"

Patrick shook his head. "The doc and Adaleigh have her resting like two hovering mother birds. And Adaleigh insists I stay in here when she's with you. I don't think it's for her propriety but Meri's, because she knows I want to see her."

David chuckled. "She hasn't seen the change I have. You're not the same man I convinced to join me and Kyle here this fall."

"You think so?" He searched his brother's face for his honest reaction.

"I absolutely do. I—"

"Knock, knock!" Adaleigh's sing-song voice interrupted. She slowly opened the door. "I hope you're up for visitors because I brought a friend."

Meri.

Patrick stood, nearly bumping the chair over. He awkwardly moved behind it in order to slide it forward. "Here Meri, sit down."

"We've come to invite you to the inn's parlor for Christmas Eve." Adaleigh looped her arm around Meri's, keeping her close to her side. They'd been staying in the room across the hall. So close, yet it seemed so far. At least Meri seemed comfortable with Adaleigh from what Patrick could tell. "We four, and your uncle, are the only ones without plans for the evening, so our lovely innkeeper, Mrs.

Holland, has given us leave to use the room for the evening. She has also left us supper in the oven. Will you join us?"

"Help me up, Patrick." David grabbed his arm. "I thought I'd miss my first Christmas with Adaleigh, and now I'll be hanged if I miss it because of a bum leg. Don't make the mistake I did and wait too long."

"Too long for...?" The words died on Patrick's tongue at the look David was sending Adaleigh, and the blush on her checks.

Adaleigh spun to the door and tugged Meri after her. "Don't be long. We even found some mistletoe."

The door closed behind them, and David tossed off the covers. "I shouldn't have come here just to earn money for a ring. Adaleigh would have me even without one. At least, I think she will."

"She will." Patrick was sure of that. But Meri ...

Meri paced the parlor as they waited for Patrick and David. She'd missed Patrick these last few days, but her body had needed the rest, just as Adaleigh and the doctor had predicted. She also needed to come to terms with her father's actions. Adaleigh had been a Godsend to talk her through everything. Now it was Christmas Eve, and she was ready to see Patrick. But what if he didn't want anything to do with her now that the danger was past?

She pressed her hands to her belly and was rewarded with a kick. Adaleigh had assured her Patrick and David's grandmother would give Meri and her baby a place to live, but what would Patrick say to that?

"It's going to be okay." Adaleigh stopped Meri's pacing with hands on her shoulders. "What has you worried?"

Meri opened her mouth, closed it. How could she explain to a woman like Adaleigh? Not only was she a confident person, she was assured of David's love for her. Meri wrapped her arms around her middle.

Adaleigh bent at the knee to catch Meri's eye. "He cares about you. I knew you required time to heal, so I kept him away. I almost needed ties to hold him back."

Meri nodded. Adaleigh had explained her plan that first night, and Meri was grateful. She had too much to think about before seeing Patrick. But now her nerves were shaking like fall leaves.

A knock and Adaleigh was at the parlor doors in an instant. Meri kept to her place in the middle of the floor as Adaleigh flung open the door and waved Patrick inside, putting up a hand to stop David under the mistletoe she'd hung over the door. With an arm around Adaleigh's waist, he pulled his girl in for a kiss that had Meri blushing.

Patrick grinned at her and made a show of rolling his eyes.

Meri bit her lip. Adaleigh had told her the story of how she and David met, and how she wanted to marry him. After that kiss, David would be down on one knee any moment!

"I missed you." Patrick took Meri's hands, turning her attention to him as his gaze ran over her as if to look for ... well, she didn't know. "How are you?"

"Better. Much better."

"Ask her, already!" David hissed from the doorway.

"Let them be." Adaleigh's whisper was anything but quiet.

Meri ducked her head and the door clicked shut, leaving her alone with Patrick.

"I have a Christmas present for you." He shifted from foot to foot. "I want to offer you a home. It's my grandmother's home, but it's a safe place for you and the baby."

"Adaleigh told me all about it. It sounds wonderful. And I'm grateful beyond words." She thought to encourage him, but he deflated a little. "Was that all?"

He shook his head but didn't look at her. Had she ruined their reunion? What else could she say?

"The baby missed you." She placed his hand against the last place the baby kicked, hoping to recreate the look in his eyes he'd given her back in the cabin.

But he pulled away. "I have nothing else worth giving you. Except ..." His face turned red and he shuffled his feet again.

"Patrick?" Her heart hammered. She had no idea what he was trying to say, but it was obviously big to him. Could she be the brave one? She rested her hand against his cheek, as he had done to her back at the cabin. It was the only other thing she could think to do, but it worked. It finally brought his gaze to hers. "Tell me."

"I want to offer you my name."

"Your—" Was he saying what she thought he was?

"I don't expect anything in return." He picked up steam, the words tumbling over one another, his gaze somewhere over her shoulder. "I have nothing to offer except staying at my grandmother's house. Not that you would want to live in a house with just me. But with my name, you and your baby would be safe from your father and judgment. It—"

She moved his chin so he looked at her again. "Tell me why."

He shrugged. "Because—"

"No." She patted his chest. "This reason."

"Because I love you."

Her jaw dropped. "You do?" He did?

"Why else?" His eyes shone with unshed tears. "It's why all I'm offering you is my name. I won't pressure you to accept anything beyond that."

"Unless I wish it?"

He shook his head, disbelieving. "Why would you—"

"Because I just might love you too." Giddiness welled up in her, a feeling she thought would never happen to her again. Not when it came to a man.

"Truly? I can't understand why."

"I think I started falling in love with you when you first realized I carried a baby. But I know I did when you felt my baby move." That moment would forever be etched in her memory, no matter what the future held.

Patrick took her hands and pressed them to his heart. "I'll raise the child as my own, because he or she is your baby. And I'll be a better father than mine or yours ever was. I promise you that."

"And I believe you." She did. Patrick was nothing like Emyr Hughes, or Leo.

Patrick dropped to one knee. "Meri Hughes, will you marry me?"

Meri grinned. "Yes, Patrick Martins. I'll happily marry you."

Patrick's eyes shown and his throat bobbed, but in an instant, he'd stood and pulled her into his arms. She had only a moment to be amazed at how he could hold her so protectively despite the baby being between them before his lips sealed their promises with a kiss. She forgot all else until the door creaked open.

"Is it safe to go in?" David's low voice intruded. "My leg is killing me."

"Hush, give them their moment," Adaleigh whispered back. "They deserve it."

Patrick chuckled as he laid one last kiss on Meri's nose, then tucked her against his side. "Get in here, brother. And greet my fianceé."

Continue the series in ...
Relying on the Enemy
Read on for an excerpt.

Relying on the Enemy

Wednesday, January 14, 1931
Crow's Nest, Wisconsin

Marian Ward battled the wind and her disgust as she pushed out of the door to the Lightning Bug, where the less reputable fishermen drank the winter away regardless of Prohibition. Never would she have considered asking for a job—and still not get one—at such a place, but she was desperate. If she couldn't find a job, couldn't heat their home, her little girls ... she shuddered, and not because of the icy wind that ripped across a sluggish Lake Michigan only to slam into her threadbare coat.

Where else could she look for work? The Lightning Bug was the last place in Crow's Nest for her to try, and without money to buy gas for the old truck, how could she drive to Hawk's River to look for a job? Were there any open positions left? Just one, at a place willing to hire a woman instead of a man. A woman with children, even if she was a widow. As times became leaner, those types of jobs became even more scarce. And how she needed one.

Tears pricked her eyes as she turned her back to the deserted lake and ducked into the alley beside the Lightning Bug. Walking home along Main Street would provide a better buffer to the wind. It hadn't snowed since the new year, making January bleak and gray. What little sunlight peeked through the overcast sky vanished in the narrow space between the buildings. However, she refused to give in to despair. Her girls, and her ill mother-in-law, depended on her. She would do anything for them.

"If you breathe a word of this ..." A hushed voice came from around the back of The Lightning Bug. Marian froze before she reached the corner and pressed against the wooden side of the building.

"I know, I know," came a second voice. Marian couldn't place either, though both were male. "You'll gut me like a fish."

"It's not a joke," the first voice growled. "If Wilson finds out, we'll both be dead."

Marian clasped a hand over her mouth to contain a gasp. Did he mean Buck Wilson, the head of the Crow's Nest Conglomerate, would ... *kill* ... them?

"Do you follow?" the first voice said. The click of a gun's hammer was unmistakable. She knew because her father had taught her to shoot. Growing up in the logging camps, he insisted she know how to defend herself.

"Get that out of my face. Of course, I understand what's at stake."

Marian's hands shook. The best way to defend herself now—and keep her girls safe—was to slip away and pretend she hadn't heard a word of this exchange. If the men knew, would they come after her? Threaten her children? Her heart pounded in her chest, but she forced herself to take one quiet step at a time, carefully backing out of the alley the way she'd entered it. Halfway to the opening on the wharf, she turned and quickened her pace.

"Hey, you!" The shout came from behind. "Stop!"

Marian ran. Steps pounded behind her as she dashed onto the boardwalk. *Think, think.* How could she blend in when there were so few people?

"Stop, you!"

She ran past The Lightning Bug, then ducked into the alley between the next two buildings, shedding her coat and hat and pitching them into a trash can at the back of the building. She turned the corner onto Main Street, scanning which building would give her the best chance at hiding. There. The milliner. It was only two doors down.

In an instant, she'd dashed inside, and held the bell above the door still to keep it from clanging.

"What's the matter?" Samantha Martins came out from behind the desk. The young single woman had secured an apprenticeship position here this past summer. "Where's your coat?"

Marian grabbed the young woman's shoulders. "I've been in here an hour trying on hats."

Bewildered brown eyes stared back at her.

Marian shook her gently. "Okay?"

"Yeah, yeah, of course." Samantha nodded, the ends of her bobbed black hair swinging. She spun from Marian's grasp and snagged two hats. She handed one off to Marian before grabbing three more. "Put that on and look in the mirror."

Marian obeyed. The baby blue hat washed out her pale face, highlighting the two pink dots on cheeks more hollow than they'd been a year ago. Her lips stood out redder than usual, too. At least the wide brim hid her windblown brown hair.

"That is not your color." Samantha rested her elbows on the wooden counter between them, in her hands a tan beret. "Want to tell me what's—"

The shop door flung open, the bell jangling like Marian's nerves. She spun, her hand pressed to her throat, not having to act an ounce.

Continue reading

Relying on the Enemy

daniellegrandinetti.com/relying-on-the-enemy/

HISTORICAL NOTE

Between the Crash of 1929 and the over-deforestation during Wisconsin's lumber heyday, most lumber companies either moved west or went bankrupt in the 1920s. Those that struggled on to the end of the decade found small pockets of trees, often far from the water and railways they usually used to transport the lumber.

As far as I could ascertain, the last functioning camp occurred during the winter of 1929. Though *Escape with the Prodigal* takes place the following year, I felt it feasible that a small lumber company could attempt one last desperate year in the Northwoods, especially if the owner employed the newer technique of replanting trees—something the Civilian Conservation Corps did once President Roosevelt instituted the organization in 1933, thus revitalizing the Northwoods to be as we know them today.

FROM THE AUTHOR

Dear Reader,

Thank you for joining me for Patrick and Meri's Christmas story. I hope you enjoyed it!

A special thank you to my Uncle David and Aunt Lois for sharing their expertise and Wisconsin lumber camp history, including stories of my grandfather. I would also like to thank Ann and Sarah for reading the rough draft of this story, my editor Denise Weimer for making this story even better and my early readers for catching my typos. And, a huge thank you to husband, my boys, and my family for their encouragement every step of the way.

Are you as curious as Meri to learn Adaleigh's story? Read David and Adaleigh's adventure in *Confessions to a Stranger*, book one of my Harbored in Crow's Nest series, where danger and romance meet at the water's edge. You can discover Mrs. Nelson's daughter Marian's marriage of convenience romance in *Relying on the Enemy*, book four in the series. Visit my website for all the details: daniellegrandinetti.com/danielles-books.

This Christmas ... an attack changes everything. Don't miss my new Christmas novella series: The Christmas Cabin. Begin with the prequel short story, *The Sheriff and the Outlaw*, in which you'll meet Sheriff Casper Yardwood two years before the events in *Escape with the Prodigal*. Read it in print as a bonus chapter in the paperback of *Escape with the Prodigal*, or in ebook. Visit daniellegrandinetti.com/the-sheriff-and-the-outlaw for more information.

I'd love to keep in touch! Join my Fireside News email community and receive a complimentary short story. Join me here: daniellegrandinetti.com/fsn. If you enjoyed the story, would you consider leaving a review on your preferred retail site?

Thank you again for reading *Escape with the Prodigal*.

Merry Christmas!
Danielle Grandinetti

Join My Fireside News

Grab a spot on my virtual hearth and receive a weekly email filled with bookish content. As a thank you for subscribing, you'll receive a digital copy of my historical romance novelette: *Fire and Water*.

Subscribe Here

Harbored in Crow's Nest

Welcome to Crow's Nest,
where danger and romance meet at the water's edge.
daniellegrandinetti.com/harbored-in-crows-nest

Confessions to a Stranger

Harbored in Crow's Nest, #1
She's lost her future. He's sacrificed his.
Now they have a chance to reclaim it—together.

Refuge for the Archaeologist

Harbored in Crow's Nest, #2
Will uncovering the truth set them free
or destroy what they hold most dear?

Escape with the Prodigal

Harbored in Crow's Nest, #3

Only a Christmas miracle will save
an unwed mother and the lumberjack protecting her.

Relying on the Enemy

HARBORED IN CROW'S NEST, #4
She's protecting her children.
He's redeeming his past.

Sheltered by the Doctor

HARBORED IN CROW'S NEST, #5
A fake relationship might keep her safe,
but will it break their hearts?

Investigation of a Journalist

HARBORED IN CROW'S NEST, #6
A second chance to set the record straight,
and rekindle a lost love.

CHRISTMAS CABIN SERIES

One cabin in the Northwoods ... a decade of Christmas miracles.
daniellegrandinetti.com/christmas-cabin-series

The Sheriff and the Outlaw

CHRISTMAS CABIN, PREQUEL
Discover the beginning of the Christmas Cabin series
in this Christmas suspense short story.

The Baby and the Guardian

CHRISTMAS CABIN, #1
A baby in danger, a man in turmoil,
and a woman determined to save them both.

The Neighbor and the Gifts

CHRISTMAS CABIN, #2

Twelve days. Twelve gifts.
One unlikely hero.

The Robber and the Witness

CHRISTMAS CABIN, #3
A simple favor, a best friend's promise,
and the end of the line.
Releasing July 2026

DI STASIO GIORNALISTE AGENCY

La Verità con Integrità. Truth with Integrity.
The Legacy of a (Girl) Stunt Reporter.
daniellegrandinetti.com/di-stasio-giornaliste-agency

Undercover Wish

DI STASIO GIORNALISTE AGENCY, #0
Alessandra Di Stasio
Chicago World's Fair: World's Columbian Exposition

Eyewitness Sketch

DI STASIO GIORNALISTE AGENCY, #1
Gabriella Salatino
Prohibition

Sabotage Games

DI STASIO GIORNALISTE AGENCY, #2

Emma Hancock
Summer & Winter Olympics: Lake Placid & L.A.

Shrouded Trail

DI STASIO GIORNALISTE AGENCY, #3
Lena Carney
Presidential Election

Fraudulent Progress

DI STASIO GIORNALISTE AGENCY, #4
Klara James
Chicago World's Fair: A Century Of Progress Exposition

Pursuing Dust

DI STASIO GIORNALISTE AGENCY, #5
Tabitha Jóhannsson
Dust Bowl

Hostile Ally

DI STASIO GIORNALISTE AGENCY, #6
Liesl Kaufman
Berlin Olympics

The Sheriff and the Outlaw: A Prequel Short Story

Two Years Earlier…
Friday, December 21, 1928□
Northwoods, Wisconsin

Sheriff Casper Yarwood peered around the giant oak tree, gaze pinned to the unsuspecting outlaw poking at his campfire in the deepening dusk. Cold air whispered of possible snow. Casper rested his palm against his pistol grip. He'd leave the weapon holstered. For now. He doubted Walter Branzon would go willingly.

Six months ago, Branzon held up the Manitowish Waters General Store. Casper had been there, could have stopped him. Should have stopped him. Except Branzon took the kind old Mrs. Holland hostage and, once he had his take, tossed Mrs. Holland at Casper. He had no choice but to catch her before she crashed into the hot wood stove.

Casper pressed his free hand into the bark of the oak, the biting pressure forcing his mind back to the present. His nose twitched against the chill. Hunting an outlaw wasn't how he wanted to spend the weekend before Christmas. But when the rumor came into the office this afternoon that Branzon had been spotted up on the northern edge of his county, Casper left immediately to track him down.

The outlaw speared a piece of meat and rotated it over the flames. Casper dropped to a crouch, weighing Branzon's weapon against his distraction. The man had proven his willingness to kill, even in front of a lawman. The memory of the two men who had tried to stop Branzon as he'd made his getaway forced Casper to rub his temple.

With Mrs. Holland in his arms, Casper had been powerless when the pair jumped Branzon, only to receive fatal gut shots for their effort.

Lord, steady my mind. Help me bring Branzon to justice.

Peace relaxed Casper's shoulders. He blew into his hands. Time to apprehend a murderer.

On silent feet, he crept forward. The moonless night providing cover. A wolf howled. Branzon raised his head, alert. Casper froze, scarcely breathing. Branzon shrugged and rotated his spit of meat.

Casper waited half a beat, then sprang. He took Branzon to the ground, tossed the stick and half-cooked meat away. In another moment, he had the outlaw trussed up like a calf, ready for branding.

"You'll regret this, Yarwood," Branzon hissed.

Casper doubted that. Never had bringing in an outlaw felt so good.

Snow fell outside as Casper led the bound Branzon up the courthouse steps Saturday morning, Deputy Titus Wilburn trailing them. Judge Cavanaugh—*Uncle* to Casper, seeing that the older man was his mother's brother—waited for them.

Their footsteps echoed in the silence of the tiled hall. Casper tightened his grip around Branzon's arm as they came in sight of his uncle's secretary. Miss Eira Mae Pryce had been working for the judge for a couple of years now. No longer in the first blush of youth, sure, but beautiful, and with a way about her that could diffuse the crankiest person. Why she remained unmarried, Casper didn't know. He had overheard more than a handful of criminals propose, not to mention the lawyers and other law-abiding citizens that had attempted to garner her attention. Frankly, he didn't understand why anyone, let alone a woman like Miss Pryce, would want to work for his cantankerous uncle.

She paused her typing as she greeted the trio, the clacking of her black typewriter falling silent. Branzon whistled. Wilburn stumbled. Casper barely restrained an eye roll at the men's reactions. "We're here to see my—"

"Uncle. Yes." She rose, poised and proper in her gray suit, and seemingly unmoved by the two lawmen escorting a murderer past. She motioned them toward a closed wooden door. "The judge is expecting you."

"Thank you, Miss Pryce." He meant only to give her a professional smile, but it warmed when her eyes twinkled in response, sending a spark of something right down to his heart. He tore his gaze away. How could he act with such disrespect, like Wilburn and Branzon?

With harsh movements, Casper shoved Branzon through the doorway to face the judge.

Judge Cavanaugh turned from the window. Dressed in the black robes of his profession, his hands clasped behind his back. "We will begin shortly."

Miss Pryce slipped in behind them, her brown hair in perfect curls under her gray hat. She set the legal pad on a straight-back chair beside the judge's desk and clasped her hands at her trim waist. "Sir, the lawyers are both expected within five minutes."

"Thank you, Miss Pryce." Judge Cavanaugh dismissed his secretary. She turned on her low heels and gave Casper and his entourage a large berth. Good. She respected the danger Branzon posed toward ...

The thought had barely formed before Branzon dropped, effectively yanking himself from Casper's grip. Branzon swept Casper's leg and Casper cleared his pistol from its holster as he hit the ground. He aimed it at Branzon, only to find Miss Pryce directly in his sights. Branzon had her trapped within the circle of his arms, his bound wrists at her belly, her arm arms pinned to her sides.

Casper's insides froze. This was a repeat of the general store robbery. A hostage situation. Casper had failed to apprehend Branzon then. Failed to recover the stolen money. Failed to save the lives of two civilians.

"Stay where you are and she won't get hurt." Branzon peered out from behind Miss Pryce's hat. While Branzon didn't have a weapon, he could easily use the binding tying his wrists to choke her. "We are going to walk out that door. If you let us go, I will let her live."

Casper lowered his pistol and Wilburn eased away from Branzon's path to the door.

"My nephew will only capture you again, Mr. Branzon." Judge Cavenaugh's stern voice came from behind Casper. Casper wanted to hush his uncle. No matter the truth of that statement, they couldn't afford to escalate this situation. Miss Pryce's life depended on it.

Branzon pulled Miss Pryce with him into the hall. "Get your paper knife, little miss, and cut these ropes."

Casper pressed his back against the wall beside the doorway, waving his uncle back. He made eye contact with Wilburn to take the shot if he had one without endangering Miss Pryce. Wilburn nodded.

Miss Pryce wordlessly severed the rope with her paper knife, not a tremble in her fingers. The rope fell away and Branzon chuckled. And then a light sparked in Miss Pryce's eye. *No, no, no.* She flipped the paper knife around in her hand and plunged it into Branzon's thigh.

Branzon howled as he yanked out the offending weapon and held it to Miss Pryce's throat.

"Drop it, Branzon." Casper aimed his pistol from one side of the doorway. Wilburn ducked low, aiming from the other side. "Let her go."

"If you don't stop the bleeding, you'll die." Miss Pryce angled her chin away from the sharp edge. "I give you ten minutes."

"And you'll bleed out if you don't come along willingly." Branzon pressed the knife to her neck hard enough to cause a trickle of blood to run down her skin. Casper worked to stay calm and keep a steady hand on his weapon.

"Certainly, Mr. Branzon." Miss Pryce winced. "Let us be off, then."

"What is she doing?" Wilburn whispered. Casper wished he knew. If Branzon got her out of the building, surely he'd kill her.

Branzon walked backward, slowly, limping on his leg. Miss Pryce closed her eyes. Closer they went to the hall where Casper would lose sight of them. Branzon's limp worsened. And then his knee buckled.

Miss Pryce broke free, but not without getting a nasty slice to her neck. Casper leapt toward her, shoving his pistol into his holster and yanking off his coat. "Get Branzon!" he shouted at Wilburn as Miss Pryce slipped to the floor, her blood dripping over the hand she held to her throat.

Footsteps sounded behind him, then a scuffle. Casper wanted to back up his deputy, but he couldn't let Miss Pryce bleed out. He cradled her on his lap, pressing the sleeve of his coat to her neck. Her breathing came fast and her knuckles whitened as they gripped his forearm.

She blinked open her eyes. "It hurts ... but it isn't too deep."

"How can you tell?" He didn't dare lift his coat away from the wound. Yet, even as he asked, he realized blood didn't soak the fabric as he expected.

Judge Cavanaugh knelt opposite Casper. "I called the doctor. How are you, dear?" His tone was unusually gentle, almost indulgent, as if speaking to a daughter or granddaughter. It caused Casper's gaze to spring toward the young woman who garnered such kindness from the gruff old man.

She pulled his hand away, and he realized she was right. The wound wasn't deep. It would need stitches and would scar, but it didn't threaten her life.

"He's gone." Wilburn joined them with a sigh. "Dead."

Miss Pryce blanched. "Did I ...?"

"No." Wilburn shook his head, and the haunted look he gave Casper confirmed it had been a choice between Wilburn's life and

Branzon's. A feeling the young man would have to live with the rest of his life.

Guilt stabbed Casper. He couldn't stop Branzon's original robbery. Couldn't save those two civilians. Couldn't protect Miss Pryce. And he couldn't shield his deputy. What kind of sheriff was he?

The question haunted Casper all weekend. By the time Christmas Day arrived, he could barely stomach the goose his aunt cooked, and it prompted his uncle to demand Casper's presence at his office first thing in the morning on the twenty-sixth.

Casper's steps slowed as he reached the place where Branzon died, and his heartbeat quickened when he reached the place where he thought Miss Pryce would bleed out in his arms.

"He's expecting you, Sheriff Yarwood." Miss Pryce interrupted his morbid thoughts. She stood behind her desk, looking as pretty and poised as she had on Saturday.

"What are you doing here?" He grimaced. "I'm sorry. I meant, how are you doing?"

Her smile filled her eyes with compassion. "I'm doing quite fine, Sheriff. Thanks to you." Her fingers traced the bandage under her chin. The injury he'd allowed.

Casper clenched his teeth and strode into his uncle's office, pulling his badge from where it was pinned to his lapel.

"Nephew." Judge Cavanaugh looked up from his papers. His brows pulled down as Casper slapped the star on the desk.

"I'm resigning." The rightness of this decision surged through him. "Titus will make a fine sheriff in my place."

The judge's scowl deepened. "Deputy Wilburn is too young to be sheriff."

"Well, I can't be one." Casper spun on his heel before the emotion that had been churning inside spewed forth.

"Where are you going?" Judge Cavanaugh's demand slowed Casper's escape.

Casper didn't quite look over his shoulder. "The cabin. And I'd like to be alone."

"I don't think that's wise, son."

Tears smarted as guilt rose with gale force. "It's what I must do." He didn't wait for his uncle to reply. He stormed out of the office, chased by the whirlwind growing in his chest.

"Sheriff!" Miss Pryce followed him down the hall. Only chivalry had him pausing, but he couldn't speak. She touched his arm. "Thank you for saving me. It made this Christmas ... Well, without you, this Christmas would have looked a lot different for my mother and siblings. You have our eternal gratitude."

Heaps of coals, those words. He glanced at the hand that touched his coat. A different coat than the one he'd used to staunch her wound. Disappearing was the right decision. For everyone. "Goodbye, Eira Mae."

She squeezed before she released him. "Merry Christmas, Casper."

Maybe someday it would be.

Casper and Eira Mae meet again in

The Baby and the Guardian

**a Christmas Cabin novella
releasing July 2024**

Find out more at
daniellegrandinetti.com/the-baby-and-the-guardian.

ABOUT THE AUTHOR

Danielle Grandinetti is an award-winning author of 1930s historical romance, where mystery and suspense intertwine with hope. Her work has received recognition including a Distinguished Faith in Writing Award, two National Excellence in Storytelling Awards, and finalist honors in the FHLCW Reader's Choice, Selah, and Daphne du Maurier contests.

A second-generation Italian-American rooted in Midwest traditions, Danielle draws inspiration from tea, books, and the creative beauty of nature. Holding a master's in communication and culture, and driven by a lifelong love of stories, she crafts tales that celebrate resilience, diversity, and belonging. Danielle lives along

Wisconsin's Lake Michigan shoreline with her husband and two sons. Find her online at daniellegrandinetti.com.